About Susan Phoenix

Healer, light-worker and psychology PhD, Susan has known great sadness and great joy as a wife, widow and mother. As a pioneer for improved deaf family dynamics and language development in Northern Ireland, she developed a reputation for her down-to-earth passion for communication. More recently she has devoted her considerable energy to worldwide research into complementary therapies to treat depression.

D1419092

This book

Jean Killen
August 2017

Susan Phoenix

Out of the Shadows

A journey back from grief

**HODDER
MOBIUS**

First published in Great Britain in 2005 by Hodder and Stoughton
A division of Hodder Headline

A Mobius Book

1

A CIP catalogue record for this title is available from the British Library

0 340 83556 7

Typeset in Sabon by Hewer Text UK Ltd, Edinburgh
Printed and bound by
Mackays of Chatham Ltd, Chatham, Kent

Hodder Headline's policy is to use papers that are natural, renewable
and recyclable products and made from wood grown in sustainable
forests. The logging and manufacturing processes are expected to conform
to the environmental regulations of the country of origin.

Hodder and Stoughton Ltd
A division of Hodder Headline
338 Euston Road
London NW1 3BH

Dedication

To Jack Holland
4 June 1947 to 14 May 2004

My co-author on *Phoenix: Policing the Shadows*, died suddenly within a few short weeks of a fatal diagnosis, just as I was completing this book. I had so wanted to be able to share it with him, just as he had continued to share his other books with me over the years, since we worked together on my husband's life story. Back in 1996, Jack had taken a brave step by agreeing to write a controversial book with me, knowing that he would be accused of many things by the authorities and those misguided souls in the paramilitary groups of Ireland. My husband Ian's posthumous influence seemed to modify his views on some of Ireland's politics, and Jack faced the criticism bravely to pay tribute to a man he respected. His stoicism was evident again in the final days of his short life as he struggled to complete his own final book.

Out of the Shadows was written to give some comfort and hope to those who face grief and loss in their lives. Ironically, it is now my turn to try to offer some small comfort to Mary and Jenny, Jack's wife and daughter.

I can only hope that Ian is not giving him too hard a time now, as they sit on their cloud together: 'So, are ya still an atheist?'

Two very brave men, both with a wicked sense of humour, who made a real contribution to the Universe.

Contents

Foreword
by Diana Cooper

I was delighted when Susan phoned to ask me to write a foreword for her new book, for I have never met anyone who radiates such love, friendliness and generosity. When I was one of her stream of visitors in France, I soon learned that a trip to the local town took a very long time, as everyone stopped to chat to her! Fun, laughter and champagne flow in her presence.

When I first met her, though, she was in a state of deep grief following the death of her beloved husband, Ian, in a helicopter crash. He was her best friend, lover and soul mate and she missed him dreadfully. In *Out of the Shadows*, Susan shares her extraordinary journey back to wholeness. Her book is filled with earthy humour and wonderful stories, some touching and some inspirational.

She paints a vivid picture of Ian, bringing him to life from the other side of the veil, and describes how her recovery was helped by his spirit, who still communicates with her. Susan also writes of how the angels often surrounded and touched her. She talks about the many people who assisted in her psychic and spiritual flowering; and she herself has become extremely psychic and intuitive. I was entranced by reading about her beautiful healing and angelic experiences. As I consumed the book, I was also astonished and humbled to read that I had been able to play a small part in helping to connect her to the spiritual realms. Thank you, Susan, for that.

Her passion for helping deaf people is mentioned, but not her selfless dedication to furthering their understanding of spiritual concepts. I remember that she attended one of my seminars in Dublin and spent the whole day signing everything I said for a deaf friend.

Susan walks with her feet on the earth and her head in the heavens. I am sure that *Out of the Shadows* will comfort many people who have lost a loved one and that her understanding and personal experience of life after death will bring hope and enlightenment to all her readers.

Diana Cooper, 2005

We have stopped for a moment to encounter each other, to love, to share. This is a precious moment, but it is transient. It is a little parenthesis in eternity. If we share with caring, lightheartedness, and love, we will create abundance and joy for each other. And then this moment will have been worthwhile.

Deepak Chopra MD

INTRODUCTION
The Journey 1994–2004

The value of silence cannot be understood except through experience. . . . What joy awaits discovery in the silence behind the portals of your mind no human tongue can tell.

Paramahansa Yogananda

I am sitting at the back of a lecture theatre in a university in Scotland – I know it's Scotland because they are all talking with Scottish accents. Suddenly I stand up and shout at the lecturer: 'Hey, you're giving my speech!'

'Oh no, I'm not,' he says. 'I'm talking about recovery and you're not, are you?'

I want the ground to swallow me up. 'Er, no, you're right,' I mutter as I slink back into my seat and pretend I'm not sick with embarrassment.

I remember that sensation of sinking into the pit of my stomach as though it had happened a second ago. I was actually in British Columbia, Canada at the time and, luckily, it was only a dream. Unluckily, however, I was giving a real talk to a large professional group a couple of days later, and the dream decided to come back to me right in the middle of what had promised to be my 'finest hour' in several years. The presentation was entitled 'Living with Terrorism' and was based on my previous life in Northern Ireland. There was interest in the topic because, of course, the now infamous September 11 of the previous year had stirred a whole new pot of thought across the Atlantic. Terrorism, suddenly, was not something that belonged primarily to 'the rest of the world'.

I should have known I was not presenting the appropriate talk when I had a coughing fit right at the beginning. Then the radio mike refused to work for the first ten minutes, and to top it all that darn dream sequence kept popping into my head. I kept pressing the power-point controller, which made the illustrations change faster than I intended. I even managed to drop my notes. You name it, I did it!

Yet after about fifty minutes the very kind audience of a couple of hundred clapped enthusiastically, asked loads of questions, and many of them came to shake my hand. Amazingly, they were genuinely grateful, despite the fact that I had felt like an idiot during most of it – so many people said thank you to me for my honesty in sharing my story. And the questions asked were not about terrorism but about how I personally had coped with the 'recovery' process – yes, there was the dream again. They wanted to know how to make a successful journey of recovery from personal, world-stopping grief.

That night I put away the Canadian talk and suddenly felt a great aversion to all the horror and negativity exhibited by my carefully prepared words and pictures, drawing greatly as they did on the earlier book about my late husband's life. What a discovery! My life was not like that any more, nor did I need to dwell on any of it other than to state: 'That's where I come from.' Positivity and good things can be given priority, light can overcome the dark, and life evolves naturally with power and renewed spirit. Forward and upwards – OK, I can get carried away with the inspiring bits, but that is partly why I can actually say I feel at peace with myself and the world today, in spite of the pain that tore my life apart on 2 June 1994. That day my husband and soulmate of twenty-eight years was killed in the worst peacetime accident ever to happen in the history of the Royal Ulster Constabulary. His death was swiftly followed by that of both my parents. Within six months I had lost my three principal life anchors, and my son too came close to death in a road accident during that horrific time.

Where does your life go when it has been shattered? I have heard this state described as being empty as a person. When all your roots and reasons for living are torn away in a few short seconds on a sunny summer day it really does seem unreal. The familiar 'This must be happening to someone else' statement made in weepy movies really is true. If the happy, fulfilled life of a loving, caring family member is wiped out, it stops your personal clock to the extent that nothing seems real for months, even years, afterwards. The sun goes in completely, and a giant shadow descends over your world.

Different people's journeys back to normality, or wholeness as I prefer to call it, are definitely a matter of each to their own. From the position of being grief-struck some take a journey backwards, others go forwards, and yet others just journey. Many find a new partner and try to re-create what they had before disaster struck. I think I did all of that (except the new partner, so far). Alcohol and drugs play a part in many people's despair. I always said no to the well-meaning friends and medics who offered so-called quick-fix pick-me-ups in the form of antidepressants, sleeping pills and the like. I felt that I knew my own brain and body better than anyone, and I wanted to stay in touch with what I was feeling without being doped and floating over the top of it. Of course, if I had a very nice glass of burgundy in my hand I discounted all of the above. Good wine is not for quaffing but for sipping with reverence. How often we had said, Ian and I, 'Life's too short to drink bad wine.' Each time I sip an excellent vintage I still say a silent thank you for the life we shared.

Today it seems normal to me, but at the time I thought how odd it was that I had always somehow known I would be a young widow. Well, forty-five seems young now, looking back over those ten years! Ian also used to irritate me enormously, when I first met him, by stating that he would be dead by the age of thirty. It was a kind of mantra that he would repeat in the early years of our relationship. 'Don't be so morbid,' I would plead.

His reply was almost always boringly similar. 'I want to live fast, die young and be a good-looking corpse,' he would say. Or, when he was feeling particularly belligerent, 'Life's a bitch and then you die.'

I have since learned the very true phrase: 'Be careful what you wish for, because it often comes true.' I must admit that I secretly breathed a sigh of relief when Ian did indeed pass his thirtieth birthday. He managed to reach fifty-one.

After his death I learned a lot about myself and a myriad of previously unexplored areas of life as I worked hard to escape that massive black shadow of grief. I journeyed back to reflect, forward to grow, with a lot of just being in the present as I progressed through each stage of my grieving and growing. If you are looking for step-by-step instructions for coping with grief, stop reading now, because I do not offer that traditional approach. Nor do I think it is helpful to look for other people or outside elements to blame for your loss. A loss is a loss, and the fact that it happens to you is not a personal punishment. How you deal with it is personal to you as an individual, of course, but there is no standard, traditional treatment for a victim of circumstance. We all have choices in life. Nor do I really care for that term 'victim', either – implying, as it does, that some form of punishment has been meted out to the loved one of the real victim, who is the dead person. In fact I think perhaps I am not into the concept of traditionalism at all.

What I do firmly believe is that we must feel the pain in order to know and truly value when it has gone or changed. We have the resources within each of us to feel and adapt to pain, both physical and emotional. If we work from within ourselves and with what the natural world and, incredibly and to my initial surprise, some of the supernatural world have to share with us, we will not only survive but learn to really live and be well again. What an amazing journey of discovery that opening up to the other realms of myself and the supernatural aspects of life has been. I have learned that the Universe is full of the most extraordinary energy just waiting to help us when the chips are down. Our own internal resources are much more magnificent than we can guess at; we just need time to access our inner self – our soul, if you like – by using patience and love. I have no idea how I would cope with losing a loved one at the hands of another; and I acknowledge that we all deal with different situations in our own way. All I can discuss here are some of the different values of this world and the next that have been clearly demonstrated to me over the last ten years since my world turned upside down.

So what is this book about? It is the recovery story that I have been asked for so many times since my triple loss in 1994. The desolation, the almost indescribable pain and the feeling of being totally bereft will resonate with most people who have suffered the deaths of loved ones. 'Lost all three at once? Very careless of you!' remarked someone not long afterwards. Yes, I laughed at the time because it is funny and rather wonderful that some great souls in this world are not afraid to joke about life and death – thank God for them, for there is nothing more sure in life than death. I am grateful for those many little witticisms that are so painfully true. In fact it is gratitude for so many different occurrences and people, plus the bizarre synchronicities of life, that fill the chapters of this book.

In 2003, walking alone along a beach in south-west France for the first time without wanting to cry, I reflected on just how long a journey it had been. Beaches were a significant part of my old life with my family. I had been happy to do many other things alone for several years, but beach walking was always very evocative and gave rise to emotions that for some considerable time I preferred to forget. As I wandered past those tall, aromatic umbrella pines, sniffing the sea air, I suddenly realised that the mnemonic for my new philosophy of life was 'GALA':

G for gratitude for all that I have learned and the kindness of so many people

A for acknowledgement of others and for being acknowledged in daily life

L for love and laughter (yes, I know it should really be a double L, but the word GALLA does not read as well to me)

A for acceptance of what life brings, no matter how it initially appears to us

It has taken me almost ten years to come to this conclusion, but I now know that I have something to share again with the world. When first invited to recount my journey, and not just the life I had shared with Ian, I was doubtful. But when asked about what my friends call my weird ideas I was less doubtful, because I know that human nature wants to confirm our inherent suspicion that everyone – apart from oneself, of course – is indeed a little weird. I have never liked the term 'normal' as applied to the individual, because it implies that there is a standard to which we all have to conform. 'Normal' is boring; 'different' is – well, different! I will share the deeper meanings of GALA as we continue, but first let me give you the background to where I found myself in 1994.

I
Life as It Was: the Railway Child

I had wanted to be a military nurse since the day I saw a young QA (Queen Alexandra's Royal Army Nursing Corps) climbing into a London taxi in her khaki outdoor uniform. Yes, I am *that* old – I remember the days when even the military women wore khaki battledress jackets, just like in the old war films. The year must have been around 1960 and I had probably been taken to London, sightseeing, on one of my dad's free rail passes. He was one of those proud Englishmen who liked his job – at least, at that time he did. We were a working-class railway family and my parents used the perks of Dad's poorly paid job to educate their children in the wonders of life by travelling everywhere possible on the annual allocation of free travel passes. Not that my older sister Pauline and I ever thought of ourselves as children from a poor household. When looking back at my childhood, the words that come to mind are cosy, loving and comfortable. In fact I could have auditioned for *The Railway Children*. Not a skeleton in sight. No groping uncles or alcoholic aunts – just loving, kind parents with a very small circle of friends and neighbours who all seemed to love and cherish us. I realise that is an increasingly odd and distinctly unfashionable admission to make, and so I will say it boldly – we had a happy childhood and we loved every minute of it.

In the springtime we picked bluebells and primroses in the woodland around the poet John Clare's village of Helpston, a short bike ride away from our terrace house in Peterborough, Northamptonshire (until, that is, the powers that be moved the town into Cambridgeshire. Amazingly, even the geography of England can be altered by the flick of a pen these days.) We would scuttle off without our parents on sleepy country roads and come home with our bunches of hedgerow flowers bobbing in the wind in our wicker bike baskets. Quite often we would have to listen to Dad quoting his favourite poems: 'Oh, to be in England now that April's there . . .', 'A host of golden daffodils' etc., whereupon we raised our eyebrows and sighed in mock boredom as children are meant to at their parents' antics. Those bluebell woods have long since been commandeered by the local crematorium, and if you tried to cycle sedately along the same roads nowadays you would almost certainly fast-track your visit to your personal urn.

Dad built us a really serious garden swing from railway sleepers – I presume yet another perk for railway workers. When the rails were renewed we were allowed to cross the common ground between us and the railway line to load a few of the old ones on to our home-made barrow. They were then magically hewn into steps, swings and all manner of household contraptions. I loved my swing. It became my haven for thinking – a serious swing for serious thinking, I suppose. Since my sister was five years older and therefore away playing with the 'big girls', I would spend hours alone, just swinging and dreaming. Mum told me many years later that Mrs Yates, our neighbour, would worry to her that 'the little gel's lonely'. Indeed, I was far from lonely. I loved the solitude, which seemed to refresh me; for, despite all the playing that children do so well, I now know that many children's energy is depleted by always having the company of other children. It is all the more evident in adult life if we do not learn how to safeguard our own energy in childhood. I loved adults and other children, but seemed to know even then that I needed 'me' time. I did spend a lot of time with adults too, as the youngest member of a family often does when the older children are away at school or work. Harry Yates, the man next door, was probably my best friend until my mid-teens when I presumably discovered boys. How differently our friendship would be viewed in this age of suspicion, and how inhibiting that we might not have been able to be such good friends today. I find it very sad that older men and women are now often viewed as a threat to young children rather than as wise mentors for developing minds.

We were the 'baby boomer' generation. The mobile and increasingly isolated nuclear family so fondly analysed and reported by the sociologists of the twentieth century was the beginning of the end for good old local support systems. When children grew up in the extended family situation of a small village or urban street where everyone knew each other and their grannies and their grannies' best friends, we young ones knew the rules. If we didn't, then someone certainly let us know, smartish. Should we do wrong we received a painless clip round the ear from the nearest adult, who then proceeded to tell our parents (or the ever-present granny). At home, our parents continued the positive reinforcement (sociological speak for more punishment) started by the caring neighbour in order to prevent our repeating similar antisocial behaviour in the future. The fact that in my case the 'punishment' was a lecture on unsuitable behaviour and then lots of love to remind me how well I was cared for seemed to work well. I think that my biggest crime was riding my bicycle too fast on the pavement, causing a risk to the local elderly population. It baffles me that so many authoritative research papers have been written about parenting and children's needs, but still ignored. Communication and love have to be part of the route to any answer.

Communication was all part of my relationship with my neighbour and cycling pal. Harry Yates and I talked about everything under the sun, and I ate my first pigeon pie in a cottage belonging to a member of his family. We had cycled across the long Fenland roads to this small, isolated house full of kind country folk where to my young mind the chat was fun and lively. I knew that Harry's wife, who was also my friend, spent more time shouting at him about household chores than discussing life in general. That was a lesson I learned early about relationships. Real communication needs to take precedence, before each individual in the relationship forms a sometimes erroneous idea of what the other person is thinking. As my dad would often say, 'If you don't ask, you don't find out.'

What a lovely person Harry must have been, taking me on long bike rides around the Fens, teaching me about nature as we went. I was lucky to live on the edge of East Anglia, with long, flat roads as far as the eye could see: sheer bliss for cycling, in comparison to the hills of Northern Ireland and the French Dordogne of my later years. I remember being taught to hang wallpaper and paint walls by my friends next door, both of whom had a lot of subliminal influence in my life. I can remember the pride when my mum and dad were brought along to admire the room that I had carefully wallpapered at the age of twelve. Thank goodness for Harry and Elsie Yates, who allowed a young girl to be a person in her own right.

It seemed I was the only one in my own family who acknowledged the household ghosts. I really do not know what age I was when I first saw the ladies who floated into the bedroom that I shared with my sister. Even then I was very aware that there was another dimension to life. I could hear the staircase creaking every night as what sounded like a posse of people trundled up and down it; they didn't seem to bother anyone else. It came as a relief many years later when I shared the same room with my new husband and he asked who they were. In fact Ian's actual words were: 'I don't know who the hell it is that runs up and down the stairs all night, but I wish they'd friggin' well go to sleep!' He just accepted this spiritual presence without further comment.

I told him about a little Victorian girl spirit, with her piled-up hair and large white pointed collar, who would sit on the end of my bed and just look at me. Each time I sat up to touch her she would fade away. There was also a lady with a rather elegant bustle on the back of her long dress. She would float across the room and appear to pick up a mirror from the dressing table, admire herself and then float back out of the door. I also explained to Ian how I used to 'communicate' through the ticking clock with whatever spirits my child's mind imagined. I would ask the clock to change beat and answer my questions by doing a different tick sequence. Interestingly, other recent conversations, with a variety of people met on my travels, have disclosed similar communication ploys between 'worlds'. I do think, for my husband, it was just one shared confidence too far – his reply to this was, 'Shit, Susan I always knew you were spooky!' These images are as clear in my mind today as they were forty years ago. There was a family joke that Mrs Wireboar, the previous owner, would 'appropriate' various spare zips and buttons that my mum needed for her dressmaking. Mum had been trained as a tailor during the war to make military uniforms and used her skills continually for family and friends. Although no one else admitted to seeing or hearing what I reported, there was an almost casual acknowledgement that ghosts could actually move haberdashery around the house.

The nightmares I experienced during childhood were, I am

now convinced, elements of the spirit world trying to make contact with me. I know I often reported to my mum that I felt like an armchair, my innocent way of describing the tingling sensation that I would occasionally experience all over my body and which made my arms and legs feel thick and muzzy. I felt like an overstuffed cushion, and as if I were outside my body looking in at myself. Before any cynical reader suggests petit mal epilepsy, it was neither that nor any other neuro-physiological disturbance, as far as I know. Certainly I was, and am, healthy enough. More holistic diagnoses can change a diagnostic picture so easily. These feelings disappeared over the years as I became more interested in serious study and concentrated on my cognitive development. I had less time to 'feel' on a spiritual level and used my brain for more 'thinking' instead. I am convinced that society's norms encourage children to pay less attention to their instinctive 'knowing' behaviour that appears to emanate from the subconscious brain, and to focus only on the smaller proportion of conscious brain behaviour. We can indeed work on a number of different planes or dimensions, without being considered a 'suitable case for treatment', once our environment allows for such ideas. How many innocent people have been inappropriately diagnosed as psychotic when relating similar symptoms, I wonder? I now know that we can travel inside ourselves to help many different aspects of our lives.

My dad really loved to travel to new horizons on the physical plane too, and would have taken us much further afield if our home-loving mum had not been so afraid of foreign ways. How they must have scrimped and saved to give us all the benefits that they could. We really did appreciate it all. Dad certainly awakened my love of difference in people and cultures. He took us on the exciting-sounding couchette sleeper trains to the South of France and the Italian Riviera. In

1966, I celebrated my GCE exam passes in Alassio when four of us, Mum, Dad, my school friend Marilyn and myself, travelled to the still pretty Italian coastal town on a railway package holiday. The first sight of those aromatic orange trees in the streets was a tonic to us all. Pauline, my older sister, now on her career path, had sent a telegram from home to tell us the results. (These were the days when we were still in awe of the telephone.) How wonderful for my parents to be able to buy a magnificent bouquet of carnations in the local market to present to me in the hotel dining room; I can still remember my squirms of pride and embarrassment. With hindsight they must have saved all year for those holidays, and spent the lot each time. They could go home and talk for weeks about the size of the peaches they had seen growing beside the roads: 'Big as your palms, they were!'

It was curiosity and wonder at all things different that I learned on our travels, be they around the local country roads in Dad's well-polished car or on rail trips to France and Italy. Interesting places and people were pointed out, games with car numbers were invented, and of course the AA man on his distinctive yellow motorcycle and sidecar always saluted our car. In those days everyone joined the AA (Automobile Association) and/or the RAC (Royal Automobile Club) and displayed the appropriate shiny badge on the front of their vehicle. We had a special bar to accommodate both badges and a 'Knight of the Road' badge which Dad had proudly gained for towing a family home when their car had broken down in the middle of the night. At the time he was driving not a car but a motorcycle, and I can only imagine the effort that would have taken as Dad did what he did best – helping people in distress. My mum often asked me to take photos of him poking around under the car bonnets of strangers in need of assistance. He loved car maintenance and was never happier than when he was fixing something in his garden shed. I also enjoyed sitting beside him, getting really oily and learning about car and motorcycle engines with their plugs and tappets as he showed me what went where. His endearing description of me, after getting involved in one or other of his projects, was 'Our old Sue is a mucky pup.' I remember how pleased he was with me for demolishing the chimney above a disused fireplace. I sat on the roof with my mini-sledgehammer and threw the debris down to him, as he really did not like heights. Come to think of it, this skill, encouraged by my father, was to come in handy when I eventually found myself alone with a fireplace to knock down in my home in France more than thirty years later. I still rather enjoy knocking things down, but never really seem to get round to building them up again!

Dad often said that money was only useful for the experiences it could buy, and was not for sitting in a savings account. I don't think it was ever a risk he took anyway. My sister and I happily discovered that he had very little in the bank when he died at the age of eighty-three. With family and friends alike he was such a generous man that money was never an issue with him. He always shared what he had by saying, 'You may as well have it now because it'll be no good to you after I'm dead – I won't be able to see you enjoy it!' After telling us just how little cash he had he would somewhat scarily add that if anything ever happened to him Mum would have to go out to work! The idea of our quiet and loving mum ever having to go out into the cold workplace always sent a shiver up my spine.

Mum's favourite saying was, 'You'll always have what does you', meaning, I presumed, that the Universe provided for our needs in the amounts necessary for our personal survival. How true that would prove to be! I valued her contributions to my life in many ways, not least the skilfully tailored clothes that she continued to make for me and my family almost until her death. She never seemed to voice her worries, and accepted life as it came. In my early childhood I had loved to accompany her as she wheeled her bicycle to the local tailoring outlet to deliver the carefully sewn and pressed uniform trousers. The tailoring would be in the basket and I would be squeezed on to the tiny kiddies' seat and instructed to hold tight to the precious cargo. It must have taken many hours of hard work, with an inquisitive little girl to handle at the same time. I don't believe I ever heard her complain about anything apart from – naturally, as is a mother's job – when my sister and I wanted to start wearing make-up and high heels at what she deemed too young an age. 'You don't need to be starting any of that business yet!'

Mum never felt sorry for herself in spite of having Dad's elderly parents to nurse through illness and her own mother living with us for seventeen years. I am sure having a gran in the house also influenced Mum's attitude to our growing up. No one ever raised their voice, and arguments just did not happen. 'We mustn't upset anyone,' seemed to be the norm. It was many years before I could hear other people disagreeing with each other without being vicariously upset. I know it sounds like those sickly sweet black-and-white movies now depicted as 'Smallsville', that cause people to yawn when everyone seems so nice to each other, but that is the way it was. In fact it was darn good to be a child star in that particular movie. I did not actively register Mum's personality during my childhood; she was the rock of stability who was always there. Retrospectively, I see her as a gentle, loving soul with an inner strength that I did not really appreciate until many years later. I have since discovered that the love and faith in people which she so clearly lived by work wonders.

2

The Scarlet and Greys

Mum's assessment of uniform tailoring was much in evidence when I eventually gained the qualifications to join the QAs, by which time the khaki uniforms had been replaced by snazzy Norman Hartnell-designed grey walking-out suits. Mum was not impressed by Norman Hartnell, and on my first weekend leave completely retailored my uniform skirt. To her well-practised eye the front was simply not up to standard. 'Can't be seen in that sloppily made skirt,' she said.

Before leaving school I had really wanted to study medicine, but I knew that the family finances would not support it. I don't think we even researched the idea of student grants or higher education since it was unknown in our circle. My headmistress discussed it with Mum and Dad, and one look at their bemused faces told me this was not to be my path. Those romantic stories of the 'scarlet and grey' heroines of the military wards seemed OK, after all. Off I went to nurse the world, become a missionary, go up the Congo and do all those idealistic things that a diet of black-and-white movies encouraged the ambitious young women of the late 1960s to aspire to. Flower power and the swinging sixties passed me by. In fact I somewhat resented the Germaine Greers of my generation who wrote their trendy articles depicting us as drug-taking, free-love addicts with daisies behind our ears. Later we were supposedly the bra-burning female liberationists who were meant to free women from the tyrannical domination of society in general and men in particular. It wasn't quite like that for me. For one thing, I liked men as friends. I didn't feel the need to jump into bed with any man who looked at me, to prove whatever point these supposedly liberated females were making. But I did enjoy male company and often preferred men's witty, bantering chat to the intense female radicalising of the time. And, at the risk of sounding pious, I had always known that I had a 'calling'. Along with thousands of others I had seen *The Nun's Story*, starring Audrey Hepburn – all that black and white kit and swooning in the arms of Peter Finch in the jungle. Yes, that was the heroic life I craved.

That was until I walked into the arms of a good-looking Irish paratrooper on one of my first visits to the NAAFI Club in Aldershot. So what can a girl do when she is young, relatively naïve and ready for adventure? She falls head over heels in love with a soulmate who seems to have been put in her path for just that purpose. Oh, the soul-searching and the thwarted ambitions! Should I tell Mum and Dad that I wanted to leave and get married and live what I had previously considered to be a boring, conventional life with the man who had never featured in any of my earlier dreams? No, the sensible thing to do seemed to be to carry on with the nursing studies that I loved and rush off to meet him as quickly as I could kick off those heavy black brogues every evening. I couldn't know it yet, but this was the man who was to make my heart race permanently for the next twenty-eight years.

When I could keep my mind off Ian, I loved everything to do with nursing. Where my career ambitions were concerned, I could never have conceived any other idea than working in a hospital in some role or other. I excelled in the caring professions, and loved it when the first person to call me 'Nurse' turned out to be Field Marshal Montgomery.

Yes, he actually walked down the main corridor of the Cambridge Military Hospital as I was scuttling off to coffee break and saluted me with his hand smartly flipped up to that multi-badged beret of his. 'Morning, Nurse.' I couldn't wait to tell my dad, who loved anything with a military connection.

Someone else who walked the corridors of the hospital was much more likely to terrorise young student nurses. The Lady in Grey, said to wander about at night wafting a chill atmosphere and a smell of violets, was supposedly the spirit of a nursing sister from the First World War. She had allegedly thrown herself from the roof somewhere above the block housing the children's ward, between wards 12 and 14. The original open walkways across the roof from where she had jumped were now covered in as hospital corridors. The lower corridors of the hospital had seemingly had their level raised and so the poor ghost appeared as footless, from the ankles up only, when spotted on the new ground floor level. Patients near to death reportedly saw this Lady in Grey near by. Other patients waiting for clinic appointments were also said to have asked about the lady in the funny old-fashioned uniform who had been sitting next to them. I didn't see this sad spirit personally, but I did feel shivers in my spine during night shift in paediatrics. The eerie sensation was increased by the sad and high-pitched crooning of a little baby with hydrocephalus during my time on children's ward. Nicola had beautifully delicate features and I loved her dearly. Hydrocephalus, more accessibly known as 'water on the brain', caused this unfortunate child to make weird crying noises when she wanted to be fed or the pressure in her tiny cranium was too much. She may also have suffered from spina bifida, which can accompany this condition, but my memory has only recalled the hydrocephalus. Later I named my own daughter after this poor little person, who I do not think reached adulthood.

As the training continued I craved the information that we learned in the classroom. I had already studied A-Level human biology and physiology with my other pals in school, some of whom went on to university. I never once felt second-class or deprived because I could not go as well – just so pleased to be given access to all this fantastic information. No one in my immediate family had been to university, so it was not a source of envy for me.

Initially, after my GCE exams and while waiting to join the army nursing corps, I had been allowed to participate in the school sixth form studies for three days each week. This was thanks to the kind foresight of the headmistress, Miss Mona Matthews, whom I well remember for her size 12 feet. This wonderful Amazon, who taught her favourite subject of ancient Greek history with style, inspired me to read and enjoy so much because of her personal enthusiasm for the Greek gods. I can see her now as she explained how the ancient Greeks used to rub olive oil into their bodies. The underlying sexual connotations made us teenage girls giggle with embarrassment and delight as this giant of a woman demonstrated the art of rubbing oneself all over with oil.

It was in the sixth form house of Peterborough County Grammar School, as a seventeen-year-old, that I had my one and only experience with a ouija board. Rumour had it that a young airman had lived in the Victorian house that had been allocated to us; he had supposedly been killed in the war (which war, and how anyone knew this, I cannot recall). One coffee break (the sixth form grown-up terminology for 'playtime') found a small group of us on our knees in the attic circling the board. Someone started to spell out questions on the board amidst an almost tangible state of tension. I don't remember the particular question, but I do remember the screams as we all ran out of a door that seemed to swing open of its own volition with an almighty crash. I have never looked at a ouija board since and I do not recommend their use in unskilled hands. This was a dangerous game for teenagers to play. When we attract spirits from the other dimension we need to know how to be fully protected, because where there is light there is also dark.

Life was not as exciting during the two days each week when I worked as an assistant in a local children's nursery. It helped supplement my income for study. My sister had left school at fifteen to work in the local railway offices and I did not wish to be considered ungrateful by lounging around in school until I was eighteen. It is no coincidence that I was to meet my first deaf child at the nursery school – I can still see the angelic blond head as little Karl sank his teeth into my forearm with the sheer frustration of being unable to communicate with anyone. How I would love to take a quantum leap in time right now and go back to help this child, who had been given no access to non-verbal communication. Karl was being blasted with sound from his enormous radio hearing aid, as was the norm at the time. The qualified teacher of the deaf in the nursery would take him to one side on a daily basis and give him 'speech' lessons that seemed to involve a lot of blowing over balloons and shouting into the microphone that was attached to his radio aid. I was not to learn about deafness and the whole political debate that surrounds the education of deaf children until almost twenty years later, and I could not have imagined at that time that I would one day be asked to spend the first two years of my professional life as a psychologist running a playgroup for another generation of Karls. Being a psychologist for the deaf did not figure in my plans any more than marrying an Irishman.

No, in those days I was determined that my dream would come true. I was all set to be a soldier and a good nurse. The *frisson* of excitement provided by my Irish boyfriend was just a passing phase, I thought.

3

Love Changes Everything

In the New Year of 1968 I was sent off to Germany for my first military posting. This was after basic training, where we really did get up at dawn and march around the parade ground being shouted at by a very stroppy drill corporal. Sometimes things happen in our lives that seem to be more than coincidence, almost as if we move along pre-ordained paths that overlap time and again. I like to call them synchronicities. The psychologist Karl Jung also used the term to describe apparently meaningful coincidences in time. In one of my life's synchronicities I was to meet this very same corporal thirty years later as a charming, middle-aged, non-stroppy neighbour in France, and we were able to laugh at her reasons for being so terrifying to us young recruits. Thirty years on, I quite understood.

A few of my colleagues earned my total admiration for being able to faint on to the cold tarmac parade ground when it all got too much for them. I have never managed to do that – what a winner it could have been, at times of stress, for added support and sympathy. However, I had managed to survive six months of ward experience, including night duty with the Grey Lady's ghost.

This was it, the big overseas posting that we had all dreamed of when first taking the Queen's shilling. It was still a shilling in those days (worth 5 pence now), and no, I don't still have the original, but I do have the little red-covered Bible that all soldiers were issued with when taking the oath to serve Queen and country. My ambition had been to be posted to Singapore – the last-days-of-the-Raj stuff that I had read about following my *Nun's Story* ambitions. It was to be more than twenty years before I visited Singapore, with my family, for our daughter's twenty-first birthday celebration. So I accepted the lesser but still exciting posting to the BAOR (British Army of the Rhine). To the British Military Hospital, Münster, to be exact. I remember how nipple-standingly freezing it was there, with weather so cold that my English-made winter coats were not up to the job.

My other memories of this freezing winter of 1968 were also of sensory origin, to do with some of my favourite subjects – food and drink. It was the first time the Peter-borough teenager had ever eaten frankfurters with chips doused in the creamiest mayonnaise and blood-warming mustard. My lifelong love of good wine was perhaps initiated there, with my first taste of German hock. I loved those tall, green-stemmed wineglasses that we all thought were really sophisticated, for hock-drinking only. I cherished a set well into the seventies, until small sticky fingers managed to despatch them to the bins of Ireland. How wonderful to explore the tastes of another culture with like-minded colleagues starting out on a new journey in life. It was not to be for long.

Before I had embarked on this momentous journey to Germany I had plucked up courage and taken Ian home, for Christmas 1967. It was a very bemused family who met Susan the career girl, now obviously madly in love with a young man who did not fit any of their preconceptions of what an Irishman would be like. My parents' only previous Irish connection had been with the navvies who worked on local building sites in Peterborough. Here was a Tyrone-born soldier with twinkling blue eyes and no sign of either a red neckerchief or string tied round his cord trousers. They were even more bemused by our proposed engagement. We had bought the simple blue sapphire ring for £28 in Guildford on a snowy Saturday afternoon that December. Ian did the officially recognised respectful thing and formally asked my dad for my hand in marriage. When Dad had deciphered what Ian was actually asking him – because his Tyrone accent was not always easy to follow – he was gobsmacked and spluttered to me, 'But I thought you wanted to be a nurse and travel the world?' We reassured him, with the confidence of youth, that the plan was that we would not marry until after my nursing studies were completed. Wrong again!

The tearful, painful and very passionate goodbyes over Christmas resulted in my returning early after only two months in Münster. Of course, where heart-racing and all that other earth-moving stuff appear in the life of a well-loved nineteen-year-old, destiny may lurk. My sore nipples had not just been due to the frosty temperatures. I had discovered that I was pregnant with our beautiful baby daughter, Nicola. It didn't feel very beautiful at the time, of course. Not only could I hardly move without vomiting, but also I had disappointed everyone including myself. The dream of single-handedly saving all the little African babies from dreadful disease was quickly disappearing. My parents were distraught with shock. Although Ian and I had become engaged at Christmas, I had convinced us all that I would become a state registered nurse before riding off into the sunset with my Irish paratrooper. This was, perhaps, one of the earliest times when fate took a hand, and thank goodness – I could have ended up as one of those dedicated career women who relentlessly pursue their own goals at the expense of all else in life. Chance would have been a fine thing. This was perhaps the first – well, second if you count the stroppy corporal – of my life's many synchronicities. The synchronicity of an unplanned pregnancy.

Luckily, at such times a loving family rallies round in spite of their disappointment at discovering that their ambitious daughter is also human. My ever-loving and gentle dad rediscovered his pride almost immediately, in time to register the marriage as that of Susan Cheshire – occupation nurse, BAOR. This esteem of all things military had only been reinforced when he was deprived of his ambition to become a marine in the Second World War: he had stayed home to nurse his invalid mother and work in the protected occupation of railway goods-train guard. Perhaps my own military ambitions had been nurtured by sitting with him to watch the Royal Tournament on television each year. I was moved by his tears of pride as he watched the massed bands, including that of the Royal Marines, both at Earl's Court and on the Armistice Day parades in the Royal Albert Hall, when he mourned not only his friends lost in the war but perhaps also his own thwarted ambitions. Throughout his life he never failed to cry at the sound of a military band, and used up many of those precious railway tickets taking his family to London to see these very British spectacles in real life. The fact that I married a paratrooper, therefore, went down well, except for a very brief but memorable interlude when Ian's pals hit the local pub for the stag night.

Everyone was fantastic, and the marriage proved to be the best thing that could have happened for us all. Our daughter was born in the little cottage hospital in Farnborough rather than at the local military Louise Margaret Maternity Hospital, which was closer to our home in Aldershot. I remarked at the time that I did not fancy my old nursing colleagues looking at all 'my intimate bits'! In fact it just seemed a nice cosy place to bring a baby into the world. Nicola took her time arriving, and delighted us all after a hard, thirty-six-hour labour that was immediately forgotten at the sight of a cute wee face surrounded by long black hair. This soon dropped off (the hair, not the face), to be replaced by soft golden tresses.

By the time that Nicola was two months old we had been posted to the sun-kissed Mediterranean island of Malta. Our precious baby had narrowly missed serious injury as our plane landed, when part of the overhead locker had fallen down – the second near miss that aircraft were responsible for during our marriage. During my pregnancy Ian could easily have flown home from a military exercise in Dubai on a plane full of paratroopers that had crashed, killing all on board. Luckily, we did not know then that air accidents and disaster in general were to play a significant role in our life together.

I loved those early years of married life on a still relatively quiet and rural island, pushing the pram along peaceful country roads where wild figs could be plucked at will. Our taste buds were developed with local spices for delicious curries and garlicky casseroles cooked with yet more wine. Those young para pals would arrive with bottles of Golden Duck and Blue Nun wine to wash down the meals that Ian loved to make for them. I think it was Portuguese Mateus Rosé in those days that moved our connoisseurship on from German hock. My palate of today cringes at the very thought, but that is how we learned to appreciate what we knew and liked. Later still, amongst the vineyards of south-west France, I learned to appreciate the skill and effort that go into making a superb wine with the help of a smile from nature. The idyllic life in Malta was not all eating and drinking, however, and our baby became a toddler on hot sandy beaches while being dangled from the arms of our young single paratrooper pals.

In that land of milk and honey and cheap booze I learned how to sober up young drunks. Too much alcohol was the only thing that Ian and I ever argued about. My problem was not with the boozing by young servicemen but with the fact that it made Ian very ill for longer than it normally took to recover from a hangover; we were later to discover that his genetic syndrome actually accounted for some of this. He and I both agreed, as we matured, that the British forces have a responsibility to teach young people in their service that there are more interesting things to discover on foreign postings than cheap drink.

Rows about this notwithstanding, we had a very good marriage. This isn't the rose-tinted spectacles speaking, but the fact that from day one when Ian went to work I couldn't wait for him to come home. I always felt excited whenever I realised that he would be home soon. We missed each other dreadfully in later years when, reluctantly, we needed to travel alone for our respective conferences or research meetings. All marriages have their times of tension and the odd fracas, of course – in the interests of an evolving and, one hopes, improving relationship. Maturity adds new and more exciting dimensions if we learn from our partners. My philosophy for any relationship has always been, 'What can I add to this? rather than 'What's in this for me?' 'Give and take works,' asserted my dad, and I couldn't dispute this – unless one side does all the taking! The resulting benefit for both partners is tangible. An old art teacher of mine, Miss Muir, once said, 'You should marry the person you cannot live *without*, and not the one who you think you may be able to live *with*.' From the day that we first met in Aldershot, I certainly did not want to live without Ian.

Once we had left the sunny honeymoon days of Malta we were again grateful for the love and support offered by our respective parents. Ian left the army as part of our quest for a more settled life. Or so we thought. We arrived back in the United Kingdom with no savings and only Ian's boyhood ambition to return to Ireland and join the Royal Ulster Constabulary. In the autumn of 1969 we spent several weeks with my family in Peterborough preparing for Ian's new role. Mum's dressmaking skills yet again supplied warm winter clothes for us all, whilst Dad's well-meaning advice reminded me that it was a big step for Ian from carefree young paratrooper to serious police officer and family man. I did not remind Dad that I too had changed directions drastically from my original ambitions. Almost continuously over the years to follow I was to need this ability to adapt, absorb and evolve.

After what was to be our first and last family Christmas with my parents and my sister's family in Peterborough I remember hearing the trill of railway engine whistles just across the road, welcoming in the New Year of 1970. But across the Irish Sea, unknown to us, dangerous civil disturbance was breaking out yet again.

4
Building Houses and Friendships

Living with Ian was never dull or boring, and our lives grew symbiotically: we were mutually dependent for our happiness over the next twenty-eight years as we grew and evolved together. We worked hard from day one to build our happy life and with the birth of five-year-old Nicola's brother, our son Niven, in 1973 we felt complete. Between 1968 and 1994 we lived first in Aldershot and Malta, in military married quarters, then moved to a suburb of Belfast when Ian joined the RUC and finally to a white-painted farmhouse in County Antrim facing the Irish Sea and distant Scotland. This old stone house gobbled up all our spare cash in the name of never-ending renovation, but became a haven for many people as well as our family for almost twenty-five years.

It was love at first sight when we saw this house, which had been lovingly built by two brothers in 1892 and had a somewhat romantic history. Formerly, it had been owned by one of the many sea captains in the area, who had returned after numerous colourful years at sea to marry his childhood sweetheart who was by now an elderly spinster. The locals liked to recall stories of how he amused himself by naming his cows after local ladies and shooting the evening meal from his kitchen door by potting his own chickens with a 12-bore. Oh, how I love such characters.

Without knowing these tales we shocked our families yet again, moving our two small children, cats and dogs into a caravan in the garden of 'The Acre' before proceeding to throw at least five years of our life into fashioning a home. Our skills were minimal at first, but we soon learned about things such as plaster stripping and, as for demolition, my time with Dad and the mini-sledgehammer paid off quite quickly. Ian had not been so fortunate, in that his dad had taught him how to hunt, shoot and fish rather than how to be a handyman; but we swapped experiences and each came to enjoy the hobbies of the other. I still love fishing, but gave up the shotgun in the interests of public relations. In fact we learned together and enjoyed it all, in spite of the delighted chortles of our friends at the sometimes hilarious mistakes we made out of sheer old-fashioned ignorance. (No, we didn't call it stupidity but I am sure others often did.)

It was obvious to one neighbour that we were in need of more practical training when he came across Ian working diligently at fixing a locking bolt to our garage door. Actually, 'garage' is too grand a name for the old cowshed that we used as a garage until it became too full of the usual junk that seems to be attracted to family life. This particular task seemed simple at first sight, although Ian never found DIY simple in spite of finding great satisfaction in it. He had carefully fixed the bolt and its keeper to the door and stood back to admire his work. The helpful neighbour waited for him to close the lock and then stepped forward to slide the door open with the lock intact – on the sliding door. 'Is that the way you do things in County Tyrone then, boy, eh?' He guffawed at Ian's lack of foresight in not realising that a bolt was unsuitable for such a job. We did our usual thing and collapsed in giggles after Ian had let fly with one of his good-natured expletives. It was a welcome relief for him to come home to the countryside, after what were often difficult days of work in war-torn Belfast, and indulge in some real physical labour. Luckily, we quickly made friends in the area – just as well, for at the beginning we regularly needed to beg the use of other people's bathrooms during the messiest renovation work. Our water was often turned off and whole rooms left bare for weeks on end. Thank goodness for good friends and neighbours.

I spent our first five years there enjoying an almost idyllic lifestyle, which I often called my 'cow-like' phase. Being close to nature and the turning seasons was immensely satisfying. I worked the land to grow all our vegetables, and raised animals for eggs and goat's milk. In those early days I bought goats from a local farmer's son and discovered the satisfying occupation of milking them for their sweet-smelling milk to be made into cheese. At one barbecue several pals thought they would like to have a go at milking our then goat, as I had often waxed lyrical about this task. The poor old nanny was ready to report us for cruelty when she had finished butting away the unwanted attention; the look in her eye saved her dignity and gave sore shins to her would-be milkers. But she was always happy to nip the juicy buds from my newly sprouted veggies as I tended the chickens, ducks and geese alongside the windswept vegetable plot. Life was good. We became a bit of a joke with our more 'townie' friends, who compared our lifestyle with that of the back-to-nature couple in the popular TV series of the time, *The Good Life*. The fact that Ian quietly lusted after Felicity Kendal, the pretty star of the show, only mildly irritated me. I find it much more irritating now when I see how well she has aged – must be the bone structure!

Another 'hobby' that Ian decided we needed to indulge in was digging our own peat, for the fire, from the turf bog high on the hills above Glenarm in the picturesque Glens of Antrim. We spent many happy family days up there cutting the peat with a special spade as used by generations of Irish families, and it was all ecologically sound. We peeled back the top, grassy turves and cut the wet peat into slices to be 'castled and stooked' and dried into hard, burnable bricks; then, as each seam was cut, the turf was carefully replaced, to allow the lovely heathers and mosses to continue to thrive. Unfortunately, what we and others were doing on a small, sustainable scale was taken over by bulldozers further south, and it began to destroy the natural habitat. There is something very evocative about the smell of a turf fire burning on a winter's evening – although how I managed to carry down two sacks at a time, slung over my shoulders, I really can't imagine now that a small supermarket bag gives me problems.

With our new pals in the area we discussed a wide variety of subjects. Perhaps surprisingly, the most fascinating conversations were in the winter months, as we gathered together our next season's seed packets and discussed the coming crops. When I see all those 'get your new life abroad' programmes on television today I have pangs of remembrance, and I do hope that the same happiness and natural pleasure will be found by those hopeful young families as they step into their rural dreams all over Europe. Living with nature and the seasons at close quarters definitely does put life into perspective. Adaptability is the name of the game. If you don't like mud, wind wrecking your hairdo or learning about local customs from local people, it's not the life for you. We both loved it. Mind you, it did feel a little like painting the Forth Bridge, and after those first five years we were ready to ease off on the never-ending DIY that beautiful old houses require.

Ian sometimes remarked upon the number of people from all manner of backgrounds who seemed to collect around our kitchen table. It started off as my quest to learn about country life from neighbours, but it went further than that. I don't know where they all came from – people have always had a tendency to enter my life at the oddest moments and for the most obscure reasons. Ian would call me the local social worker, because neighbours who had not previously social-ised with each other tended to meet in our kitchen to chat. Twenty years later, a French neighbour made the same assessment of my home in France. Another new friend recently labelled me a 'lighthouse', with people travelling along my light beams – an interesting analogy, I thought. I am grateful for good friends, but right now I am hiding in my new Spanish home in case a similar influx happens here!

In the 1980s I had no intention of going into any kind of paid occupation, as I really believed that our children needed their mother to be at home when they returned from school. I know I was in the lucky position of having a salaried spouse and I would probably have had to think differently if Ian had been unemployed. However, we did not have a high income in spite of popular belief about policemen in those days. Ian was already thirty when he joined the police at a very basic salary more suited to an eighteen-year-old. But we loved to invite guests to dinner or for the weekend just to share the family life that we enjoyed so much, and Ian never actually grasped the concept that doing so depleted the family fi-nances. He preferred to suggest, somewhat less than subtly, that it was my 'voluntary' work with all kinds of needy groups that was the problem. This ongoing banter as to who was at fault for our almost permanent insolvency carried on for most of our married life. He always felt that I was undervalued, no matter where I chose to devote my skills. I am not sure why he came to this conclusion, but suspect it was because I was rarely paid even in later years when I was working in a more professional capacity. His frequent teasing claim was that he supported a lot of the deaf population in Ireland from his pay packet.

It was as a result of meeting my profoundly deaf neighbour that I became involved with deaf people and their families. She would pop over to ask me how we were coping and gradually taught me sign language so that we could communicate on a more meaningful level. It was to be another unexpected tangent in my life.

I look back on a life full of people and love interspersed with a lot of life-threatening danger. As Ian rose through the ranks of the RUC he became one of the key figures in charge of anti-terrorism. His military experience, strategic planning ability and robust sense of humour appeared to be an asset in the dangerous war against terrorist activity in Ireland. His more senior colleagues did not always appreciate his forthright manner and his habit of calling a spade a shovel at high-ranking planning meetings, but Ian was not interested in currying favour with the bosses. He saw his job as that of making Irish society safe for each individual, no matter what their religion or politics, to live without intimidation or fear. In simple terms, he cared about his country and he respected the men and women who worked with him irrespective of their rank or background. His ability to see the funny side of some of the most bizarre situations endeared him to many of his colleagues. Those who did not always recognise his humour admitted to being a little scared by his deep voice and often very blunt way of expressing himself. Many years later the Chief Constable of the RUC, Ronnie Flanagan, confided in me that had Ian only been more diplomatic he too could have held that post. My reply was, 'Yes, I know, but he wouldn't have been Ian!'

During those years, when policemen were being killed in what appeared to be permanent open season for anyone in a uniform, we became accustomed to using anti-surveillance techniques on our way home to make sure that no one was following us. Conversations in public never mentioned 'the job', in case a would-be terrorist was listening: 'the job' was more a way of life that permanently affected the whole family. At the time of publishing Ian's life story in 1996 the media had become preoccupied with what they considered our odd way of life. It was only then that I started to realise just how different our life had been from that of the rest of the world. The press seized upon things that we had come to take for granted. They liked the idea of my hiding Ian's gun in my handbag when we went out socially, so that he could remove his jacket in public. They reported the surreal incident when we had heard a knock at the door in the middle of the night and Ian asked me to cover him with the shotgun from the top of the stairs while he opened the door Starsky and Hutch-style, holding his pistol high. The fact that this was only a friendly knock from a colleague delivering a pay cheque that led to us collapsing in helpless giggles of relief was overlooked by the sensation-seeking news headlines. The image of me lying at the top of the stairs in my nightgown holding a shotgun was quite bizarre, I suppose.

It was about this time, in the early seventies, that Ian decided he wanted to buy some pyjamas. I wondered if he were suddenly becoming prematurely staid and proper. However, it was nothing of the sort; it was because the IRA (Irish Republican Army) had developed a nasty habit of blowing people's heads off in their bedrooms in the middle of the night. The doorbell would be rung when everyone was in bed, and one's natural instinct was to look out of the bedroom window; once the curtain twitched the gunman would shoot whoever was there. Ian had decided, one, that no one in the house should ever look out of windows when the doorbell went and two, (in his words), that the bastards would not get him when he was naked.

Our friends became our extended family, and we valued them all equally. We felt that we had learned to value friendship and comradeship as young marrieds, far from home, but we were sometimes disappointed when in our new civilian life some new friends did not reciprocate the way we felt. In close communities, where extended families are still living near by, there is a boundary of friendship with others: although that friendship is warm and caring, it stops short of the love shown to those who share blood ties. I have never been frightened to use the L word, whether it is love for family, friends or a specially enveloping occasion that inspires the feeling. I suppose the word 'friendship' covers the affection felt at some level, but real comradeship and love involve putting the needs of others before oneself and it does not seem a bad philosophy to me. A silly philosophy, perhaps, if one does not learn to be discriminating in the giving and also to protect oneself from exploitation, but with reasonable common sense it usually works for the good of all concerned.

I have never liked the word 'private' – usually, in my opinion, a pseudonym for 'lonely', 'cold' or 'indifferent'. We did wonder, however, if we were a little too open when we declined to put 'private' signs on our house drive. On one occasion I arrived home to find a family picnicking at the bottom of our drive in our field. I merely smiled as I drove up to the house, as they were doing no apparent damage. Five minutes later the mother and child arrived at my door to request a fill of water for their picnic kettle. I duly filled the kettle, but went back indoors chuckling to myself as I realised the child was clutching a bunch of my gorgeous daffodils, gathered from the verge on their way up the drive. I hoped it would add colour to their town house and that they would extend the same hospitality to another family one day when someone picked the flowers from their front garden!

It was important to us to share our family life, and indeed our love, with many people throughout the year and not just at times like Christmas. We only ever shared one Christmas with our own blood relations, but in subsequent years we know that we gave pleasure to many lonely young men and women who were away from home in December. After Ian's death I was so delighted to hear a young man whom I had never met saying how sorry he was about my husband's early death. Taking it initially as an expression of sympathy, I thanked him but told him not to worry about me. 'Oh, no,' he replied. 'It's not that. You see, I was always told that if I was ever in Northern Ireland on Boxing Day I was to make sure to get an invite to Ian's house, as everyone told me it's famous for the best Boxing Day hospitality in the world!' What a back-handed tribute to hear at such a sad time. It really made me chuckle – even more so because of his embarrassed expression when he realised what he had said.

We always had a 'shooting day' on 26 December. It had started as a wild game shoot along the local braes beside the sea, and the bag was subsequently cooked in the evening for a game dinner. However, as our more sensitive souls evolved we developed it into a clay-pigeon shoot and the joke of having roast clay pigeons for dinner became replaced with an anything-in-the-freezer feast. I say this not just to suggest that we were ecologically enlightened, but because over the years we developed an aversion to shooting little fluffy, furry things. We invited all manner of individuals to our home on that day, more so than throughout the year, because we really felt that we could never know when we too might find ourselves alone in an alien place. I am now so glad we did so, because I have had cause to be very grateful to the many people who have extended the arms of friendship and camaraderie to me as a person alone in recent years. How true is the saying, 'What goes around comes around.'

I know that the lifestyle we enjoyed in Northern Ireland was not typical of the way of life of most people during that awful period of 'the Troubles'. It was certainly very special. Like us, our children had friends from all sides of the community (in Northern Ireland parlance that means Catholics, Protestants and people of no particular religious faith). It is difficult for people living in other countries fully to understand this preoccupation with the religion of another person. I love to quote the story of the young Buddhist visiting Belfast who was asked by a group of friends what religion he was.

'I'm a Buddhist,' he replied.

'Yer, we know, but are ye a Catholic or a Protestant Buddhist?' they asked.

I loved my life in Northern Ireland, and was privileged eventually to be able to work all over the island with deaf clients and their families from many walks of life. On one of my home visits I was a little taken aback to be asked directly for the first and only time about my religious beliefs. Having driven many miles along windswept country roads to help out during some crisis or other, I was standing in a cosy country kitchen chatting to the mother of a girl with whom I was doing a social skills training programme. Suddenly the broad accent of County Tyrone rang out: 'So what are ye, anyway?'

When I realised the significance of the question I gulped and stuttered, 'Er, well, I'm English actually,' and that put me firmly in the 'nondescript' religious camp.

As a young mum in a Belfast suburb I had helped in a

church youth club, where again we encouraged youngsters to attend no matter which religious or irreligious background they came from. As another of life's tangents I had become involved in prison visiting and driving the families of prisoners to see their loved ones. These activities came about because of my friendship with the local vicar's wife, a spirited, intelligent woman and way before her time. She managed to get us into all kinds of scrapes as we drove the youth club minibus to collect families from under-privileged areas of Belfast and escort them to the various sadly over-crowded prisons of Northern Ireland at that time. I recently met Elizabeth Jones and her husband Eric, the then vicar, as they drove down to southern France to celebrate their joint eightieth birthdays. Neither of these two good people looked any older as they joined me for a good glass of Bergerac wine to talk over the old days. I gratefully acknowledged their profound, loving influence on my life all those thirty years before. I had been a lonely young mother with a small child and I needed something useful to do in the community while my husband was risking his life on a daily basis in trouble-strewn Belfast. Although I was never a conventionally re-ligious person, it seemed natural to turn to the local church to ask if there was anything that I could do. Eric and Elizabeth soon found plenty to take my mind off what might have been happening to Ian, and it proved to be cheaper and certainly more fun – though far more exhausting – than tranquillisers.

In the interest of supplementing the family finances I took on an evening job as a slimming club organiser – even if people would not think so to look at me now! I really enjoyed those evenings, which started after I had tried all those other part-time jobs that young mums do if they don't want to leave their children in the care of strangers. I had given up on touting the party plan stuff, from Tupperware to sexy undies, round the local housewives, mostly because I spent more time listening to the common problems of loneliness and frustration than actually selling anything. The slimming club answered some of those needs in the community by becoming a group therapy for all manner of problems, only some of which were related to excess pounds. The local club became so successful, growing from only six members to over eighty weekly, that I asked my employers for permission to split it into two nights a week. Each of these then quickly expanded to the original high numbers, with the next progression causing me the famous working mum's problem of guilt. I found myself running three successful slimming clubs as well as helping with the local youth club. The weekly weigh-ins developed into 'agony aunt' sessions, with me hearing all the would-be slimmers' problems as I knelt at their feet to take a note of the pounds lost that week. The combined smell of sweaty feet and tears dropping on my nose was not what I had planned in my modest quest to supplement the family finances. Although I could see that a lot of the weight problems were really 'life' problems – indeed, the mind, body, spirit problems that I still deal with today more holistically – and that these women needed a listening ear, I could feel my energy being sucked from me in many ways. I suppose this was my first real view of how one's mental state can affect one's physical body. Although I enjoyed feeling useful in society again, I also began to resent not being at home with Ian when he was there. I actually liked the fact that he worked shifts because we could spend time together when other nine-to-five families were working.

The birth of our son solved all these problems in one fell swoop as all my energy was diverted back to where it was happiest in those days. I refocused on the family, and limited my community work to the weekly youth club. The voluntary staff there were committed people with whom we had a lot of fun. Nearly thirty years later I still hear from some of those young people who attended the club and came to consider my family as their friends. Ian would come along to help out too when he had free time, and was particularly useful when we went on annual camps along with the children. His job was the one that no one else wanted to do – emptying the latrines.

The interest in youth work initially developed in that very open and modern-minded church youth club was to encourage me to look again at the needs of local communities when we moved out into the countryside of County Antrim. When we had managed to put the roof back on our new home Ian suggested that I develop my growing knowledge of young people's needs by going to university and studying for a degree in youth and community work. But even this did not work out as we had expected.

5
Happy Pills: To Pop or Not to Pop?

I am often asked if I ever worried about my husband's life, as his job always seemed so dangerous. Of course I did, but to allow such a worry to take over my life would have defeated the whole purpose of living. I also sought to allay any negative effects for the sake of the children: to have allowed them to know that their dad was at more risk than most of their friends' parents when he went into work each day would have been counter-productive. I saw my role as being there to give them as normal a childhood as possible; in this context I interpret 'normal' as meaning happy and loving, as all childhoods should be. There is a family joke about my rather over-protective warnings: seemingly, 'Be careful – you could put your eye out with that!' was one of my favourites. To this day there is much mirth if I even hint at the presence of some danger in the vicinity. 'Look out, Mum – that could put your eye out!' they chortle cheekily.

I think nurses, especially, are often over-cautious about their children's wellbeing because they have seen at close quarters the weird and unlikely damage that children can do to themselves. As a nurse I saw a very broad cross-section of illness and injury in the young, because the Cambridge Military Hospital received sick children with special problems from all the British military posts across the world. That is my excuse for knowing of, and fearing, the worst – but hoping for the best – at all times. Ian and I felt that our mission was to take very opportunity to love, share and enjoy our lives with our children and friends, because who knew what tomorrow might bring. Hindsight tells me that we kept ourselves too busy on a variety of 'projects' to dwell on danger or fear – we often stopped ourselves in our tracks and demanded why we were doing something, or how we had got involved in yet another 'good idea at the time'.

It is all to do with being a good bluffer and not letting the world know when you are scared, because there is little to be gained by infecting others with one's own nerves or fears. I fully acknowledge the individual personality differences that lead us all to cope with life trauma in our particular way. Personally, I find it more useful to try and convey comfort to another person by showing a calm demeanour – even if my own knees are shaking beneath my jeans. So if that is being dishonest – so be it. Perhaps I could have been a good actress if my legs had been longer! In everyday life, when we learn to put on a front we start to absorb this act internally, so in the end we may come to believe it ourselves and get on with whatever needs to be done. This is the basis of mind over matter. But such 'acting' can be dangerous when there is a real need for outside help and to conceal such a need would be self-destructive. Some people may well need a little initial pharmaceutical help before they can respond to other thera-pies, but it takes some very skilled and experienced profes-sional work to recognise this subtle difference. It also takes real personal bravery for the sufferer to know that it is time to look for help. The British stiff upper lip is not always helpful – in fact it is sometimes absolutely stupid. However, there is no real pharmaceutical 'happiness' that can be injected or popped into mouths crying out for help.

I truly believe we are here to experience fully everything that the world has to offer. I know that coping behaviour differs from one individual to the next, but there are extremes: I have known young mums, for instance, who popped off to the doctor's surgery because the budgie died or their partner was late home a couple of times. And unfortunately one only needs to cry in front of many stressed-out, although caring, GPs and the pen is already poised over the prescription pad. All too often the tearful patient is sent home with supplies of whatever tranquillising drug is currently fashionable. Some of these mums I came across were placated for a short time – sometimes the doses were increased or combined with a vodka or two, and the zombie syndrome commenced. Many people are, even today, living as though in a sleepy dream. I believe that GPs of the seventies and eighties were responsible for more (legal) drug addiction than many of the (illegal) pushers of today. Those antidepressants were of a different chemical group – the tricyclic antidepressants as opposed to today's supposedly 'safer' SSRIs, of which Prozac is an example. Will Prozac do similar things to people today?

In 2004 a healthcare survey conducted by Norwich Union revealed that eight out of ten GPs admitted to over-prescribing antidepressants. Alarmingly, three-quarters of the GPs questioned stated that they were prescribing more such drugs than they had been five years earlier. Psycho-pharmacology is a rapidly developing science, but to prescribe drugs without a limited timespan and supportive therapy is dangerous and unnecessary because so often when the drug is stopped the symptoms return. Antidepressants do not 'cure' depression in the way that antibiotics cure infection: they just put a lid on the psychological symptoms, encouraging more evident physical illness to appear in the body as the soul cries for help.

When I hear about children and vulnerable young adults being tranquillised through chemical intervention, I shudder.

If more time and funding were made available for real mind, body and spirit treatment – the holistic approach – I am certain that many millions of pounds would be saved in drug purchase by the health services. It is not a big secret that the pharmaceutical industry courts doctors with the freebies of corporate hospitality to seduce them into prescribing around £9 billion worth of drugs on the NHS annually. The money saved could help to adapt holistic therapies to work in tandem with the conventional medical services. More cash to raise existing doctors' salaries could also counteract the aggressive marketing of the drug companies. There must be a remedy for the UK's exhausted medical services.

If frightened and vulnerable people are merely sent home from the doctor's surgery with a prescription and no other support, it is more than likely that they will return for top-up prescriptions. Three million people in the UK are currently swallowing antidepressants on a regular basis – people are becoming dependent on drugs that no doubt many of them did not need in the first place. If, on the other hand, short-term drug support is offered to restore chemical balance to the neurotransmitters (brain chemicals) while techniques for coping and remedial help are offered long-term by skilled, accredited therapists, there is a higher chance of full recovery. Meditation, for instance, can help depressed people under-stand that negative, self-destructive thought patterns are often fleeting and can be dealt with given time. There is no doubt that changing your perceptions can make a huge change in your personal reality. You don't have to change the world, but with the right support you can change yourself. Holistic approaches can indeed help the individual to know and accept all manner of life problems and then to deal with them effectively.

The usual reply from the authorities to pleas for such

therapies is, 'But we need scientific proof.' It is already out there by the bucketload (that is my best scientific jargon) in medical and psychiatric journals from all over the world. We need to combine the best of ancient wisdom with the best of modern medicine. As with all new and controversial perceived threats to professional worlds, the evidence of good practice will remain buried or the innovator will continue to be scorned by his or her colleagues until enough caring people stand up to be counted.

From the tabloid press upwards, evidence has been reported not only that healthy people are happier than sick people but that happy people are healthier than unhappy people. Happy people have happy thoughts that really do cause distinct changes to the neurotransmitters that in turn improve the physiological wellbeing of the body. Forget happy pills – try happy thoughts. But I shall leave the proof of this discussion to later chapters, in which I describe my own trip down the long and lonely route in quest of help.

You may wonder why I am so emotional on the subject of over-dosage with tranquillising/calming drugs. It is partly because, in the final years of his life, my father was slowly reduced by his doctor to a drug-dependent semi-invalid. My mother was powerless to do anything to help as he was prescribed more and more antidepressants for a physical ailment that started off as Ménière's disease. This debilitating disease of the inner ear causes severe dizziness and nausea, often giving the appearance of drunkenness. To this day it is a difficult case for treatment and takes time to resolve. To watch a loved one who has been the rock of the family slowly and surely deteriorate to a chair-bound condition, detached from the world, is heartbreaking. At least when people are actually feeling emotions, whether fear, anxiety or great happiness, they know they are alive. I now know that we need to experience the lows in order to appreciate the highs properly. Modern society and the professions have tried to remove emotion from our daily lives: the term 'emotional' has become a dirty word. But a life without emotion is a life without soul. This need for emotion to be shown was exemplified by the outpouring of public grief after the death of Princess Diana. Were these people really grieving for a princess or was it an excuse to get in touch with their own emotions, that the British stiff upper lip mindset had buried for many years? I personally feel that emotional outbursts are often triggered by an outside influence that allows the individual to express their hidden feelings under another guise. I know that when Diana died we cried as a family all over again, for Ian's loss.

Life often needs to be put into perspective for the individual to value his or her lot. My poor father was numbed into a state of just existing rather than living his life to the fullest potential. This was a man who had always valued the simple pleasures in life. He was not in any way a religious person, yet he always knew what was right and good in life. He would sit down to a traditional Sunday lunch at home, or in later years in a restaurant, and say, 'Don't you wish that everyone could be enjoying such a great meal?' My sister and I learned our gratitude subliminally, without lectures or pontificating. Dad eventually became unable really to enjoy anything other than the basic acts of daily life – eating and sleeping for most of the day and smiling benignly at his family, almost like a child. He occasionally woke up to have warm and interesting conversations, but mostly he appeared numbed. My mother did not complain, but did that marvellous counting-your-blessings thing that seems to help many people if they can get through the mire to it. She would say, 'Well, he was a good man. We had good times together in the past, and no one can take those away from me.' Never once did she lash out at the real problem – the inadequate medical support services. She would not have been aware of the term 'holistic medicine', but if she had she would surely have known that my father could benefit from it.

How I would love to go back in time to help my dad out of his inertia, undoubtedly caused by over-prescription from an unwitting or overworked GP. We owed so much to this fun-loving, intelligent, kind husband and father. Ultimately it was the medical professionals whom he had so admired who slowly and surely put his very soul on to the back burner. In hindsight, perhaps there was some other inherent problem that had triggered and then exaggerated his Ménières disease. Was it the boredom or frustration of a middle-aged man who had not been able to fulfil more of his life's ambitions? I will never know. I do know that there are many people in a similar situation today whose family and friends may feel it's none of their business to interfere. But can we afford to leave it to political correctness or drug companies to run today's world? We can make a difference if we really care.

Mum's own resilience and stoical courage were wonder-fully demonstrated when she herself was dying, within months of Dad's death, and in considerable pain. As she was cared for so tenderly by the nurses of the Macmillan Foundation and the Sue Ryder hospice in Peterborough she was offered painkilling drugs on many occasions, but often refused them until her final days. The staff were amazed that this dying old lady, who had watched her husband deterio-rate from drugs, would sometimes reply, 'Oh, no, thank you. I wouldn't like to get hooked and become a junkie.' Mind over matter indeed.

Ian and I had many conversations about such matters, not

least because he really did believe in mind control of physical ailments. I did not always appreciate his philosophy, especially when I was in full labour during the birth of our daughter and he looked sincerely into my pain-racked eyes and said, 'It's all in the mind, you know!' When it came to recreational drugs such as cocaine and heroin, he prophesied that they would become a very big problem in Ireland. During his early years on the beat on the streets of Belfast he witnessed many drug-induced incidents. His prophecy that the Irish terrorist organisations would become the drug godfathers of future generations has indeed come true since his death.

Many more of his wise suggestions have slowly become fact. One of those was, 'You'd better get a recognised qualification because you'll need it one day.' It was at his instigation that I went to study at the University of Ulster (then the Ulster Polytechnic) – yet another plan that started off on one track and developed a tangent all of its own. I had chosen a part-time degree in youth and community work as a result of my earlier youth club interests and my growing concern for young deaf people. However, during the first year we were shown aspects of several different courses and I began to realise that I would like to study psychology. There were several reasons for this. Perhaps the most traumatic for me – in fact for us as a family – was the fact that doing youth and community studies involved spending three months on a kibbutz in Israel. When I was about sixteen I had seen that beautiful Paul Newman film *Exodus*, with all those bronze-legged kibbutz-dwellers clad in khaki shorts, and had thought what a great experience it would be. But thirteen years on, the prospect of leaving my cherished family to do I am not sure what in the name of 'study' for such a long time seemed ludicrous. The female lecturer looked at me pityingly as she completely misunderstood my reasons for declining the placement and inherently the degree course. 'Frightened to travel alone, are you, dear?' Far from it, but I just could not see how I was eventually going to help in a so-called social care organisation if I neglected (because that is what it would have been in my mind) my own happy, stable family unit. There was no compromise, so I left.

When Ian and I reviewed my remaining choices we both knew that psychology was my niche; he probably knew it before I did. I liked the idea of combining my earlier studies in the field of medicine with my interest in people and the increasing amount of voluntary work I was doing within the deaf community. We also now knew that it would be practical for me to enrol as a full-time student. I had observed just how flexible lectures and seminars were, and also how many hours young and single students could spend in the students' union. It was simple: they went to the bar, I went home. I had the somewhat misguided idea that I could read and peel potatoes at the same time. It didn't quite work out like that, although eventually I managed to fit in the deaf community work, feed the chickens and the children, be Ian's attentive lover and best friend – oh, yes, and read the odd book when I wasn't writing essays, of course. Yes, it fitted our new tangent and not a happy pill in sight.

6

All Good Things Come to an End

When I achieved my first degree I was over the moon that I would never have to read another book for anything other than pleasure – or so I thought. I had managed to adapt my studies to help inaugurate several new services for deaf people in Northern Ireland, and as a result I had met many interesting and committed people from all walks of life. Many of these good people gave their time freely to help with basic adult education projects for profoundly deaf sign language users, social skills training and drama for deaf teenagers, and guidance/counselling for the parents of profoundly deaf children who needed sign language to communicate fully with their families. Happily, what they had started was continued by appropriately trained and paid staff. When I eventually registered for a PhD researching family intervention with deaf children, I was generously donated research premises in the local school for the deaf. It was even more useful that this happened to be just next door to the University of Ulster – my luck was in at last.

Such luck slightly compensated for the highly charged atmosphere that surrounded all areas of work with deafness then, and continues to this day. I would often return home quietly fuming after attending public meetings about the lack of provision for deaf sign language in education or some other much needed service, and was continually amazed to find that some members of the caring or educational professions were clearly working not for the good of their client group but rather for the next step on their personal career ladder. In my innocence (or stupidity, some would say) I often got into trouble by being the one stuck with the political hot potatoes that were handed to me by some professionals who knew the correct course of action but were frightened that following it might jeopardise their own career plans. Being without a career plan – or any plan actually, except to do something useful – in my innocence, gullibility, call it what you will, I would stand up in public and say what we all knew to be necessary and true. Those audible 'tuts' still ring in my ears. Of course, the colleagues in question would afterwards deny all knowledge of having fed me the facts from their case studies that matched my own research. If you have seen the film *Braveheart*, when Mel Gibson as the Scottish hero William Wallace turns to his supporting armies on the field of battle to find they have all deserted him, you may remember that superbly desperate expression on his face that just said 'Oh shit!' How I sympathised. Ian and I often asked ourselves just what we were in training for as we discussed our life lessons over a good bottle of wine on a regular basis. We both felt that we were here in this life to learn something – but it was often extremely difficult to discover what it was we were supposed to be learning. Even carefully draining the swamp seemed to leave us up to our backsides in crocodiles!

Campaigning conferences and meetings about deafness used up a lot of energy in those days. Later, I discovered just how useful the campaigning skills learned in this scenario were when I had to use them in a very different field. I am now more certain than ever that each hard knock comes into our life to teach us something that will be absorbed by our inner self to be used later, in this life or the next.

My strong, supportive husband, who was no stranger to

boat-rocking in his own work, suggested that I should be more assertive in the campaigning area. I in turn suggested that perhaps he should employ a little more subtlety in his approach to policy-making by his senior officers. We both appeared to be fighting an almost constant battle in our respective areas as we sought to contribute to the change that is needed for development to take place. How much easier we could have made life if we had just accepted the status quo and minded our own business! Ian often told me that the skills developed in negotiation now would help me elsewhere in later life – little did I know . . . I wonder, did he?

But despite the struggle in my chosen work with deaf people and their families, the majority of my colleagues were great people and I shared some equally great moments of satisfaction with them. A sense of humour seemed to be always in evidence. The pleasure of working with a group of deaf and hearing friends for a common cause was hard to beat. Meeting deaf adults who had been poorly educated and encouraging them to come on board gave me a great sense of achievement. When we eventually started making educational videos, the generosity and ingenuity exhibited by local businesses and other educational groups was very welcome.

Empowering someone to blossom as they recognise their own abilities is always satisfying. As part of my work, in 1990, I went to America to interpret for a deaf colleague who had won a Churchill Travelling Fellowship to study technological communication for deaf people in the USA. A charming American lady, the widowed mother of a deaf attorney in New York, offered us accommodation while we had meetings with her son. When I asked her how she coped with life alone, just as so many people now ask me, her reply was, 'All you need in this life is someone to love and care for, and something useful to do each day.' Not bad philosophies: now, from experience, I can confirm that they are a good starting place when rebuilding your life. Quite amazingly, I knew then that one day I would be in her position as a widow. I also recollect her room full of photographic collages depicting her family life before her husband's death. As I glance at my own family photos that I felt it necessary to arrange into happy collaged memories fourteen years later, I wonder whether subconsciously I thought about her as I tearfully clipped and snipped my way to what I once would have thought a very weird comfort. I even asked a newspaper journalist not to include that particular 'therapy' of mine in one of her articles about me, as I thought it made me sound like an even weirder old lady than I was!

During my early married life I met two other women who each lived alone, and on both occasions my instincts told me that later I would have a life like theirs and be without my partner for a long time. I don't know where these intuitions came from – they entered my mind in an almost subliminal way. One was an elegant middle-aged lady who lived in a neat, tidy Irish cottage with a beautiful garden and imma-culate furnishings. Such style, and the sense of peace, made it an oasis to the busy mum and working wife that I then was. I thought to myself how nice it would be to have such a neat place to live in. I also mentally noted that I would not trade my clutter of children, dogs and country life at that time, because one day I would miss it all no matter how stressful it could be now on a daily basis. The future loss was already part of my consciousness. *I KNEW!* The other woman, a social worker for deaf people, had been widowed for a few years when we met at a conference. She lived quite alone in a tower block in a particularly unfashionable and rowdy area of London, and when I asked her why she had chosen such a potentially dangerous place her reply was that she was needed in the community as a friend and advice-giver for so many of her more needy neighbours. She died of cancer a few years later, but what a precious jewel she must have been in her lifetime. She really did love, and was loved in return, long after losing her husband.

By the time that Ian had survived into his thirties, in spite of his premonition of dying young and his nasty habit of participating in life-threatening incidents in the Belfast battle for peace, we lived a busy life full of fun, laughter and excitement, even though there was always the *frisson* of danger in the background. Ian had been promoted to sergeant and then inspector. He was well known for both his quick temper and his sense of fairness, tempered with a robust sense of humour. Not that I always appreciated the humour. On our seventh wedding anniversary, when he was a force training officer based in Belfast, he came home holding something conspicuously behind his back and telling me that I would always remember this night.

'Why?' I asked excitedly, because it was rare for Ian even to remember such dates, let alone make a fuss for me.

'Because I need you to use your artistic talents and draw a sub-machine gun on here,' he said, producing the blackboard from behind him. 'It's for tomorrow's weapon training lesson.'

I should have known.

On another anniversary I actually received a card from him while he was away from home. He had been promoted again by this time and was on a counter-surveillance course, being taught how to follow crime suspects without being detected. I was so shocked that he had remembered that I gushed my loving thank-you to him over the telephone.

'Oh, you're very welcome,' he said. 'I just happened to be

on a surveillance exercise in the town and I was trying to not look suspicious in a card shop, so I thought I'd buy a card for you.'

Romantic as ever. It was his earthiness, accompanied by that tongue-in-cheek humour, that I loved about him. No false compliments or words that did not mean what they appeared to. When Ian said he loved me, I knew he meant it. His gruffness concealed sentimentality and kind-heartedness, and the twinkle that accompanied his direct style of speech was hard to resist once people understood his sense of humour. He was indeed a strong and sexy character, with a charisma that he never quite understood himself.

Many years later someone who had been a young constable with him on duty in Carrickfergus in County Antrim told me how he had been introduced to Ian's form of policing. Gangs of youths would traditionally congregate on the evening of 11 July each year during the Orangemen's marching season, and these illegal groups often ended up in bother. One year, Ian, accompanied by the young constable (an ex-paratrooper like Ian) and a part-time policewoman discovered a gang of over fifty youths stoning the local Catholic church. The young constable had just been hit over the head by a flagpole, causing a wound that later required fourteen stitches. Ian turned to the young man, who was dazed and bleeding, and said, 'Have you got your baton with you?'

'Yes, sergeant.'

'OK, let's get this lot dispersed then!'

As usual, the Phoenix method of dispersal was direct and determined, and around fourteen rioters were hospitalised – one for every stitch in the young constable's head. The two-man baton charge was considered a great success, although local Loyalist leaders were never too sure whether Ian was really a Protestant policeman or not. When the ringleaders were arrested some of them turned out to be local councillors, and Ian was greatly amused by their outlandish claims that they were just out that evening 'investigating reports that the policemen had been throwing milk bottles at innocent Protestants'. The culture of the police service has changed since then, though only partially for the better – these days, Ian himself might have been arrested!

This direct approach to hands-on police work continued even when he was later promoted into plain-clothes work and then finally to a key role in counter-terrorism. Fellow officers have since spoken to me about his forthright manner and how terrifying he could be in meetings when he spoke his mind. Ian did not believe in beating about the bush – diplomacy was never his middle name. 'Life's too short to piss about,' he would often say. Did he know, in his case, just how short? However, his sincerity could not be doubted, and his commitment to peace in Northern Ireland was equalled only by his belief that the individual in Ireland had a right to live a full life without intimidation and fear in their own community. He despised terrorism, and criminal behaviour that he felt masqueraded as terrorism, in his country that he loved. Ian was an Irishman in every way, but he felt that there must be a united Northern Ireland living without fear before there could be any effective discussions for a united state of all-Ireland. This unusual and balanced reasoning challenged the media stereotype of a Protestant policeman in Northern Ireland. Ian felt a united Ireland was feasible if terrorism was conquered and if the twin populations of the North could only accept each other. He did not think it was a good idea to pander to terrorists from either side of the political-religious divide. In his eyes, a crime should be punishable by the law, and not by 'gougers', as he insisted on calling the street thugs who terrorised their respective communities.

In those years we also discussed our feelings about death and our personal ideas of the afterlife. We would walk the mountain paths of Northern Ireland together or wander along the beaches wondering whether we would ever have the time to do more travelling. We often sat on a mountain-top after a strenuous climb and discussed life in general. Ian's colleagues were being killed and maimed on a regular basis in the 1970s and 1980s, and after each young life was cut short we would re-express our gratitude for our continued happiness together. In fact, since Ian's death friends have told me that they found us irritating because we obviously enjoyed each other's company so much and because our idea of pleasure, when we were not walking the mountain paths and beaches of Ireland, was a night in together with some good music and a decent bottle of wine. We coined the phrase, 'Life's too short to drink bad wine' without realising just how true that would be. We valued each precious moment together, and I often wonder if anyone ever found the odd errant champagne cork that flew through the air on those hilltops as Ian sneaked a bottle out of his rucksack – 'Just to toast the good things in life,' he would say as we flopped down after a hard climb up our favourite Irish hills. When we shared our home with friends they remarked on the warmth and hospitality, which I am still proud to offer today to friends and strangers alike.

So we passed twenty-eight years together in the blink of an eye, as they say in all the best stories. The first eighteen months and the last were rather similar, if I am really truthful. Those passionate, fun-filled early days, before marriage, grew into a deep, respectful, mutual love for each other, our family and life in general. Ian and I learned to enjoy at best and survive at worst whatever life threw at us. We really were each other's best friend. Our *annus horribilis* came about twenty-five years later, to take the shine off Ian's fiftieth birthday and our silver wedding celebrations. 'Never become too complacent,' should perhaps have been our motto.

We suffered two of the worst years of our life because of a misguided combined plan to help someone out and to go into a business venture. Altruism in business is fine once there is a sound financial basis, but someone needs not only to know how to do the books but also to be able to understand audits done by another person. Ian and I both trusted my profoundly deaf business partner's original audits, and proceeded to plough our meagre savings and a bank loan into a business to help develop a whole new area of technological assistance for the Northern Ireland deaf population. When the partner left me holding the worst financial problems we had ever known it was all hands on deck and the family rallied round. Our loyal daughter gave up her burgeoning career in radio journalism to help out – a decision that the whole family felt guilty about for many years. The ever-dedicated and kind Nicola proved to be a highly skilled business manager, just as she had excelled at her other professional roles. Sadly, it was not to be enough, as we continued to make losses in the delicate balance of cash flow. We ended up with as many debts as my original business partner, if not more, a huge bank loan and an intelligent, well-educated daughter pulled away from her much-loved career path. Total frustration all round.

Somewhere in the middle of all this we learned that we were on the IRA hit list, and therefore needed either to move house or to install massive security to our home. Ian also discovered that he had a genetic syndrome that could have shortened his life considerably had he been a smoker. It was, luckily, one of the vices he did not have, but it was none the less very distressing to learn that his two brothers had died early as a result of this undiagnosed condition.

What did we learn from the whole sorry mess? We learned many things – that we were not cut out for retail business, that we should value the love and support of our children even more than we already did, and that in spite of all that life had dealt us we could pay our debts and bounce back. This we did – for six short months.

We had taken out a massive bank loan rather than file for bankruptcy. It would perhaps have been easier to take the latter route, but we were very aware that had we done so other small businesses would have lost income too. It seemed fairer to us to pay the business debts and move on. I settled back into my consultancy with deaf people and their families, while trying to raise funds to produce more educational videos for deaf children. Our daughter went back to her radio journalism, our son entered his final year at university and Ian continued with his fight against terrorism. Such a glib statement makes it sound as though Ian went back to cleaning windows – but that is exactly how we survived. We all knew that there was a job to be done, and accepted the fact that Ian was in a particularly dangerous arena. The whole family felt that Ireland deserved to be rid of the dangerous groups who controlled their respective communities by terror. We had a great deal of respect for the men and women who risked their lives on a daily basis to help the individuals, of whichever political or religious affiliation, to live a life without intimidation or fear. The fact that Ian was one of those good people gives me a great deal of pride to this day.

To celebrate our return to 'normal' and Niven's twenty-first birthday all four of us went to Goa for a holiday in January 1994. We had made a similar trip, to Singapore, five years earlier to celebrate Nicola's twenty-first birthday, and had decided that travel parties beat cake and candles every time. Our love for the Far East had been fostered from that time, and happy memories of that last family holiday are with us for ever.

In May 1994 I finished the production of a pilot video about famous scientists for deaf children in sign language. It was to be launched in a local hotel, and coincidentally on the day that I went to plan the launch Ian was having a business lunch there with some security colleagues from England. As a surprise he asked for me to be paged, and as I entered the dining room there was a mutual flash of excitement as our eyes met. It was an emotion as powerful as when I had first met him as a young paratrooper twenty-eight years before in Aldershot. How happy we were to be back on track again . . . or so we thought.

7
As It Was

It was the date that I will always remember – unusual for me, as I have a great problem with numbers and dates. This was not the way I would have chosen to improve my memory, but 2 June 1994 started much the same as any other summer morning. Ian and I sat chatting in the sunny kitchen over breakfast. We would usually start our conversations as we woke, simultaneously indulging our senses in that beautiful, dreamy, sleepy lovemaking that comes so naturally after twenty-eight years together. The conversation would continue into the bathroom and ramble on to the kitchen. More often than not Ian would pinch my expensive face cream and ask the same question, 'Is this stuff any good?' I would retort as expected, 'Yes, and it's too good for your old beard – use your own!' Which of course he never did – just to annoy me (amazing how long my creams now last in my solitary bathroom!).

As we ate our last meal together, he looked across the lawn to the scruffy little shrubbery in the far corner. 'What's that red flower over there?' he asked. I was equally surprised to see a spot of colour waving amongst the evergreen collection of weeds and thistles masquerading as ground cover until I could get the few hours that I had promised myself to sort it out. After I had kissed him goodbye I ambled across the lawn, breathing in the sea air and counting my blessing as I went. Yes, life was good: unusually for the Ulster coastline the sun was almost shining, we had paid our debts, the bank loan was going down and I had a holiday to plan for next Monday. Ian would be coming home for lunch before flying off to a weekend conference in Scotland. I was due to take the car over and meet him in Inverness, after which we planned to visit all those friends in Scotland and England who had been begging us to stay for longer than I could remember. I picked some of the little red bells that Ian had noticed, from a plant that I had been talking to somewhat redundantly for several seasons. This was the first time it had ever responded to my coaxing – I was beginning to think that perhaps Prince Charles's belief in talking to plants was misguided in my case! I popped the flowers into a tiny vase on the kitchen windowsill and promptly forgot about them until many days later.

It seemed as though I was no sooner at my desk, and trying unsuccessfully to book a ferry to Scotland and a flight to Manchester for a conference about deafness at the university, than Ian appeared home. 'I'll just get changed and do a bit more glazing before we go to the airport,' he called merrily on his way up the stairs. Now 'glazing' was all too grand a word for his ongoing task of cutting up old glass and fixing it into his latest 'project' – a sun-lounge for the dogs! At least that was what he had labelled the wooden structure he had been working on for several weeks. I had actually weakened and helped him paint the wooden rafters on a very sunny Monday, only three days previously. It had been a wonderful day, with lots of teasing and a picnic lunch on the patio. The patio had been another of our 'projects' – Ian had long since moved on from putting sliding bolts on sliding doors to amuse the neighbours. We both loved working outdoors together on what became known as 'Dad's Follies'. It was our relaxation, although we used to muse that we would do better to pay professionals to do the jobs properly. If we had done so, though, I would never have learned to make such a great concrete or cement mixture – my muscles at that time would have made a weightlifter proud! I always seemed to be the labourer, but rarely complained as the fringe benefits were good.

So there he was again, destroying more good materials in the name of DIY. We ate lunch while he talked about the coming conference. He had not wanted to go at all, as he felt it would consist of the usual talking around solutions to potential problems rather than tackling them head-on as was his style. His sincere reasoning had not changed since those earlier days as a policeman on the beat, and he had been proud to be the last uniformed policeman to do an unarmed foot patrol in the IRA-controlled West Belfast. Once the government had given in to the crime lords by allowing 'no-go' areas in a supposedly civilised society, he always asserted, they were well on the way to allowing terror to rule. He felt that the peace process was being wrongly managed by civil servants who could not understand the Irish accent, let alone the Irish psyche, and certainly did not understand the criminal mind. But what he thought made little difference anyway, since the only people in a position to make a real difference were Englishmen in a government that was totally fed up with the Irish problem, and who could not hear a balanced voice over the political debate.

When we had eaten he continued to work away with his latest pride and joy – a brand-new glass cutter – and I popped outside at regular intervals to remind him that he had a helicopter to catch. Eventually he came to the door of my office with a wicked gleam in his eye, growling that he was late and demanding to know why had I not reminded him. I abandoned yet another call centre answerphone and did not book the ferry to Scotland. As we raced out to the car we decided it would be better for me to wait until he came back when we could set off from home together on the Monday, rather than my making the long drive up to Inverness to meet him. 'Pity you can't come with me in the chopper,' he said. How right he was.

As we drove along the County Antrim roads towards the military airport at Aldergrove the weather had turned to its more normal grey, with hill-hugging clouds. We discussed my latest ideas for raising funds to provide an all-Ireland video production service for the deaf community and their families. Statutory funds were limited, and would not be forthcoming since sign language was being actively encouraged in educational provision. I had been fund-raising for each video as we produced them, and it was becoming a wearisome chore. 'Why don't you write to Richard Branson? He's a man of vision,' Ian suggested in one of his brainwaves, and I agreed that it might be worth a try when we came back from our holiday. We chatted about life in general, solving the world's problems as I drove. When we were in the car whoever was in the passenger seat would tuck their palm under the thigh of whoever was driving. It was a comfort habit I was not conscious of until many months later when, without thinking, I did the same to my daughter as she drove me somewhere. Then, it was no longer a comfort.

As we approached airport security I slowed down and Ian discreetly moved his hand to wave his ID card at the security guard. We passed several Wessex helicopters that I had thought were for the RUC group. 'Nah,' said Ian. 'Not those wee baby ones for us. We're using a Chinook – you know, the jungle stuff!' I could tell by his voice that it was the trip he was looking forward to rather than the conference. As a young paratrooper he had always rather liked jungle warfare, and this trip was to take him back to his youth. He had described the helicopter journey to me after the previous year's conference, which had been held on the Mull of Kintyre. He loved to make the *wop wop wop* sound of a helicopter approaching, and we both thrilled at the opening shots on the *MASH* television series where the American medics rush to meet the choppers as they land. In 1993 he had brought home the Argyll and Kintyre Ordnance Survey maps, to show me where one day we would go for a rambling holiday in the heather. I was not to know that very soon I would ramble without him in that heather for a far different reason.

I dropped him off outside the hangar where he would board the bus to be ferried out to the waiting Chinook. He kissed me and gathered up his suit carrier (actually bought for our son's twenty-first birthday six months before – 'Nice present, Dad – just what you always wanted, eh?') and his small leather rucksack that he used for hiking and business meetings alike. I watched him walk off to join his colleagues from the RUC, military intelligence and MI5 who were already climbing into their orange immersion suits, required by military regulations for flying over water. As he loped away I admired his back: he had a distinct walk, casual but with a military straightness, his broad shoulders and silver hair sitting well above the narrow waist and hips that belied his fifty-one years. His loving smile of departure as he closed the car door would have to suffice, as I knew that he would not turn and wave – he never did. 'You just go forward – don't waste time looking back,' was his motto. I did indeed wish that I had been going with him – I too liked the idea of the exciting helicopter ride and helping him to fish between meetings with the folding rod he had borrowed from a friend. As usual, my heart turned over as I lost sight of him and I pulled away to drive into Belfast to dine with our daughter.

Nicola and I chatted and joked, enjoying each other's company as always. I told her I would let her know when we left for our road trip after the weekend, and she wished me a good holiday. Eventually I headed for home, and as I followed the road north I turned to BBC Radio Ulster on the car radio. Then it came – the kind of news flash you never ever want to hear in your whole life: '*A military helicopter has crashed on the Mull of Kintyre in Scotland while carrying security forces personnel to a conference in Inverness – first reports suggest that there are no survivors.*'

Looking back, I can see I had a stereotypical reaction – it can't be true – and then I heard myself screaming, 'No, no, no!' As I clung to the steering wheel I became aware of people in a car in the outside lane staring at me, and it suddenly struck me that I was still driving and in a very dangerous manner. I looked desperately around for a telephone box – these were the days before we all had a mobile stuck to our ears. Nothing was available apart from a heavily guarded police establishment just ahead of me at Greenisland. I pulled in beside the fortified security box and demanded to be let in to use the phone. I can still see the shocked faces of the men on duty, who must have been wondering what this deranged woman wanted. I don't think I looked like a terrorist, but then who does?

The rest of that day became a blur as the earth-shattering news became clearer, but isolated incidents stand out oddly in my memory: the facial expressions of so many good people trying to do their best for a woman who was in no state to think or do anything for herself; and the station sergeant as he used the phone to try and get information that was public knowledge before anyone in the police knew. Good old media again in a bid to be first – all sensitivities go to the wall. I knew that he knew they were all dead, but he pretended and so did I. Then there was the poor chap who was allocated to drive me home in our car – he crunched the gears a lot, and I remember feeling sorry for him with his totally messed-up passenger wittering on about possible hospitals on the Mull of Kintyre and whether survivors could be visited this weekend. I recall the children's faces and those of our friends as they met me at the door – no one had known where I was. Both Nicola and Niven had arrived from Belfast before me. At some stage I swore at someone and felt immediate shame at my outburst – for what, I cannot remember. And there were all these people saying, 'Put the news on. . . . No, she mustn't look. . . . She'll do what she wants anyway!' Who were all of these faces in our home – and where was the only face I wanted to see right then?

It was eleven o'clock at night before an official report and a list of the victims arrived at my house in the hands of two of Ian's devastated colleagues. Twenty-eight men and one woman had died instantly as the giant helicopter hit the Mull of Kintyre in the area of the lighthouse known as Beinn na Lice, Scottish Gaelic for Hill of Stone. A giant fireball enveloped the heather as body parts were sprayed over the hillside. Ian's last helicopter journey, that he had so wanted to enjoy, had taken him much further than his youth as a soldier.

Three days after the crash, numb and wrapped in my pain, I insisted on visiting the crash site. I had in fact begged to go earlier, but it seems to have been regarded as an odd request. I can't understand why the powers that be were so shocked that a widow and her family should want to see exactly where their husband and father had died. If it had been a road crash or some local happening I would certainly have wanted to see the place, to be where he had physically finished his time on earth.

The two RUC officers who had been despatched on the

night of the crash to oversee the site and the bodies were waiting for us as the plane landed. I shall never forget Trevor and Paul's faces as I alighted from the little Islander plane at Macharanish airfield with my two children and a close friend. Why did we, as a family, feel the need to comfort these two strong policemen? But we did. Hoping they would never have to witness such atrocity again, I asked how they were coping. 'You know, Susan,' said Trevor, who knew Ian well, 'Phoenix would have loved this place we were in last night. We had to get ourselves a drink in the local pub after the worst day of our lives – and there must have been a wall full of over a hundred single malts. He can choose a place to die, eh?' The wonderful black humour that had sustained Ian and me through many bad times in recent years, and continues to sustain Northern Irish people in the face of ongoing political confusion, came to the fore then. My reply was that I now knew why Ian had been so late coming back to me that terrible night – he had been hovering over Trevor's shoulder having a last connoisseur's sniff of his favourite Scottish malt whiskies.

This, when I look back, was one of the earliest comforts that life (or death) provided for me: not the whisky story, but the fact that I had already felt Ian's spirit come back to me the night after his death. When I related the story to these two stoics and several other kind people whom I met later I couldn't read the expressions on their faces, but I always had the feeling that they thought grief turns women a little mad. Perhaps if they were to meet me now, ten years on, they would have their suspicions confirmed! It had been a long, harrowing evening. Was it only a few hours? It seemed like a lifetime of pain already, and more than a little unreal – just as it is described in those well-meant books on pain and grieving. Luckily, our souls have the ability to distance themselves from intensely painful moments, and at such times it really does feel as though one is looking into another person's life. I was not sure whether I was in the bubble looking in, or inside the bubble looking out.

On the night Ian died the children and I went to bed just to try to escape the pain. I can't remember if anyone stayed in the house with us. I do remember pacing my bedroom, looking out of the window occasionally to see a wispy, eerie fogbank floating across the sea from Scotland, and wondering how I would ever sleep again. As I lay on the bed, at around 4 a.m. I suddenly felt wonderfully happy and peaceful and glowing from an unexplainable, all-pervading energy, with a silly smile on my lips. 'This can't be right,' I thought. 'Ian's dead – why should I feel like this?' The best description for the feeling was electrically charged cuddles. The next day I asked the children how they had slept. 'Well,' said Nicola, 'at about four this morning I suddenly felt wonderfully happy and peaceful and glowing with a silly smile on my face – it felt wrong, knowing that Dad's dead.' I asked Niven if he had felt anything. 'No, Mum, I slept – but sure you know that Dad would know it would take more than him to wake me up!' We all laughed, maybe in some hysterical, grief-stricken way – all I remember is that it sustained us for some time. Such moments of laughter and oblique hope became lifelines to us as a close family group, and many of our friends shared that feeling with us. What's that old saying, 'Laugh and the world laughs with you, cry and they all clear off'?

The cause of the crash is unknown; requests for further enquiries continue to this day. Two young special forces (SF) pilots were unfairly made scapegoats when there was insufficient evidence to allocate blame or determine what happened. SF pilots are dedicated RAF pilots who fly the SAS in worldwide operations. It awaits someone with dignity and honour in the government to clear the pilots' names officially and restore their reputations, in order to allow their families to move on with pride. Ian's death remains an enigma.

8

After the Crash

As I stood at the kitchen window a few days after the crash I glanced at the little red flowers picked on that last morning that Ian had been alive. My friend and colleague Gloria slipped her comforting arm around my shoulders and told me their name. 'Seven drops of blood,' she said. When I told her that they had only flowered for the first time the day that Ian left she put her hand to her mouth, aghast.

'Oh, no, Susan. I'm so sorry – I didn't mean to upset you!' As if she could, with her compassionate smile and selfless help. That plant never flowered again. In fact it disappeared completely from the garden before that summer was over. Seven drops of blood indeed.

My heart felt emotionally torn out, and the physical pain in my chest lasted for longer than I can remember. The autopsy had said that Ian's heart had been torn out in the impact. His face had been untouched, and he had not burned as so many others had. Phoenix had truly risen from the ashes. Now I had to try to do the same – alone.

In hindsight, the house full of people was one of the things that came as a surprise to me. Over the years, Ian and I had discussed death because of his high-risk occupation. I had always said, 'If anything ever happens to you, I'm not having one of those Irish wakes where everyone comes to sit round the coffin for days. I shall lock the doors and grieve in private!' As was often the case when I made one of my pompous, all-knowing statements he just smiled and said

73

enigmatically, 'We'll see!' Of course, the reality of a situation inevitably takes precedence over theory and people arrived *en masse*. They actually wanted to be there. Fantastic friends and family just turned up with massive hugs of comfort and everything they could carry just in case it was needed. The things that I most remember, oddly, were toilet rolls and coffee. How thoughtful, and how do people automatically know what will be most needed? All that coffee-drinking – and, of course, the crying – used up millions of loo rolls. Old friends whom I had not seen for years arrived with hugs and funny stories to remind us of the good times we had shared with so many people over the past twenty-eight years. Have you ever noticed how at such times everyone hugs, strokes and touches each other without inhibition or judgement, people doing what they do best – giving love and comfort? At times of grief we need physical contact. Look at any funeral party and you will see arms being patted or gently stroked, hands held and those all-embracing body hugs that can be a lifeline for the sufferers. There are always those who find it difficult to hug someone else, but they often feel able, in the face of such obvious emotional pain, to give of themselves in some small way. For many, just holding the hand of another person is a big step. Tactile behaviour reminds us that there is comfort out there – just as the well-loved baby knows it is safe when held, so does the suddenly isolated adult need that physical reminder that all will be well again. Of course, at the time one cannot conceive of ever feeling happy again. I just felt empty and numb.

Just a simple question from my solicitor, who asked me the age of my parents when he was trying to estimate how long I might live, stunned me. He unwittingly gave me a shocking insight into what appeared to me at the time a dark, lonely, forty-year-long tunnel. At that time I couldn't perceive even a faint glimmer of light at the end. Even now, I can still feel how his innocent words burned into that heart-wrenching, searing physical pain of being bereft.

My children matured ten years almost overnight, and suddenly became the carers. The all-encompassing love we felt for each other and for their father was tangible. How difficult it must have been for them. I often ask myself if I neglected their grief as I was thrashing around in my own head, searching for some kind of anchor or even a bit of sense. I think that we hugged each other as a family for hours, but I still wonder if I gave them enough comfort. I know that they were the only reason I could see for remaining on this earth at the time. Their loving support and robust, adult sense of humour sustained me. I can still hear their own personal pain in my head. In spite of it they were able to stand at our house door and greet all those hundreds of visitors, whether it was the local postman, government ministers, neighbours, close friends or family – I gratefully stored in my memory the equal respect with which Nicola and Niven treated each one. Ian would have been so proud. One thousand five hundred people attended his funeral and, surprisingly, we found that we knew, or knew of, most of them. What a rich life we had all led together. Almost five hundred people came back to the house, spilling out of doors into the garden and the drive outside. Most were carrying a bottle of champagne. The local off-licences were reportedly sold out of Moët and Chandon for days afterwards. Ian's pride would have been boundless.

We decided to scatter the ashes over the braes below our house, where Ian had been happy to walk with his family and his dogs. On the day of the scattering I found it very hard to move from the sofa in our lounge, but lay there clutching the ugly brown plastic pot masquerading as an urn containing the remains of Ian's body. The funeral parlour had asked if we had an urn of our own – now where does one keep that kind of thing in a happy home? It was a minor detail at the time, and not what one ponders about in the middle of grief, but I do think something more suitable than what looks like an empty salt pot could be provided as standard. As the house filled with friends who were to accompany us to the hillside I remember only too well the physical pain in my chest and my tears as they soaked the sofa. My Scottish friend Christine popped her head round the doorway to see if I was ready to join the rest of the mourners.

'Do you think you can die of a broken heart?' I asked, seeking words of comfort.

'Aye,' she said, 'you can!'

At that moment I would have been happy to go too, but I still chuckled at her Scottish version of tact and comfort.

A few days later, when everyone had gone back to their lives, another old friend came to take me to Sunday lunch. John, despatched by his wife Diane to escort me to their house, found me sitting sobbing, as was the norm, in the little office at the front of the house. Kneeling in front of me, he rocked me tenderly in his arms. John too had suffered great loss – a baby son and a teenage daughter – so he knew the pain. 'Susan,' he said gently, 'I just want to tell you that the pain you feel today . . . Well, it never goes away and you'll suffer for ever!' I actually burst out laughing – because, knowing and loving John as I do, it was so typically him and meant as a comfort. With such good friends, what can I say? I appreciated all of those little gems that made me laugh amidst such intense grief. In fact I think I preferred such help to the 'You're so brave' kind of comfort, because your real friends know that courage is the art of trying to be the only one who knows you're scared to death.

The reaction of my parents to Ian's death surprised me. They were both in their eighties, and as they had been too ill to attend the funeral Niven drove Nicola and me over to see them a few weeks afterwards. Their inability to offer any comfort came as a shock, yet with hindsight I understand. You always expect loving parents to be there for you during the worst times. This time, though, it seemed that they themselves could not cope with the trauma. They behaved as if everything was normal, apart from dear old Dad saying, 'I don't understand why Ian had to go before me when I'm ready.' That was it. There was an air of nothingness in their normally cosy, caring home. After hugging them both I had to leave, and Niven stoically drove away with his deranged mother sobbing and almost screaming on the back seat as Nicola patted my hand and tried to be strong for me. Since that time other people have told me that they have experienced similar reactions from elderly parents after the loss of a loved one. Is it because they themselves can feel their own soul getting ready to depart this earth? I wonder.

The children and I tried to warm up our own souls by sharing fun and exciting moments in those early months. We dashed about travelling, sky diving, sailing – many of the things that Ian would have loved to do with us had he ever been able to afford it. We got on with our lives as best we could Both children started new careers and made new friends. I was so proud of them.

Gloria turned up with a present for me. When I opened it there was a pair of brand-new walking boots, but not in my size. She grinned cheekily and told me that she knew I would miss my hiking days with Ian and she intended taking over as my walking companion.

Encouraged by the ever-faithful Gloria I had gone back to do some work, sporadically, for deaf families all over Ireland. It had felt very satisfying running workshops for the parents of deaf children, who needed so much support. However, I knew that I did not have enough mental stamina to give of my best to such families at that time. It is difficult to provide a supportive psychological service when you really just want to shout, 'I'm in pain too!' or, 'So, you think you've got problems?'

Doing things alone for the first time turned into a series of milestones for me. During one of the Dublin workshops for deaf children I was staying in a town centre hotel and discovered that room service solved the problem of having to walk into a hotel dining room alone. Although I had of course dined alone on business trips, it was different now and I felt vulnerable in my detached bubble of unreality. One of the ways in which I experienced the grieving process was that it seemed almost impossible to concentrate on any written media. It was many months before I could read a book for any useful length of time. So I thought, during this Dublin trip, that I would go to a cinema very close to the hotel. It sounds a simple enough exercise, but I quickly realised I had never in my life walked into a cinema alone. Panic set in as I paced backwards and forwards in front of the cinema, which was showing a film I really wanted to see. In the end I shoved my hands into my coat pockets and marched up to the kiosk to ask for a ticket; within seconds I was inside, feeling as if the whole world was wondering what I was doing alone in a cinema. Once I had calmed down I looked around and saw that people do actually go to cinemas alone and they are not just the dirty raincoat brigade. Since then I have even gone to London theatres alone when I have really wanted to see a play. There is a feeling within society that, unless you are part of a couple, you are of little value or just a 'sad person', and I have spent some time coming to terms with that attitude.

Because of this I have also tried to change my own personal perceptions of others. I now try to make eye contact and acknowledge the lone diner in the hotel with just a smile or a nod to let them know that someone knows they are there. Many people are perfectly happy in such a situation, but I am always aware that some may be in the position I was in ten years ago and I am prepared to risk a dirty look if there is a chance that some comfort may be passed across.

Of course, I wasn't always doing things on my own. I started to take Nicola and Niven to places that Ian and I had wanted to be able to show them in their teens when we had holidayed without them. We had often said, 'Wouldn't the kids love this place?' and it was good to share these experiences at last.

There was more heartache around the corner, though. My mother, diagnosed with cancer of the womb three years earlier, had seemingly made a successful recovery in her usual stoic manner, but then had a recurrence. Shortly after Ian died my father was taken very ill and sent to hospital for tests. It was late summer when my sister rang to ask if I could come to Peterborough to talk with the hospital staff. Both parents were in wheelchairs as I held their hands and the ward sister explained to my dad that he had advanced cancer of the prostate. It had not been diagnosed earlier because of all his other drug-induced symptoms. The continual prescription of antidepressants and tranquillisers since the diagnosis of Ménière's disease twenty years previously had produced a variety of side effects, including facial tics and muscle aches. He had always had back pain that had been labelled as psychosomatic; this time it was not in his mind – it was killing him. I held their hands tightly, trying to comfort both at once, but they just sat in stunned silence until my dad said, in his usual pragmatic way, 'You'd better give me a tablet now, then. I'm ready.'

'Oh, no, Mr Cheshire. Don't be like that – I'm sure you'll have many good days yet,' stammered the sister, stunned at such a direct request for euthanasia.

By the time my sister had returned from the Burghley horse trials, where she had been for a well-deserved day's break from looking after our ailing parents, Dad was ready for his final journey. We had chatted about nothing much, but his big question came out loud and strong as his eyes cleared dramatically.

'I wonder what it'll be like to be dead!'

'I really don't know, Dad,' I replied. I only knew what it was like to be alive without the dead, and that was hell for me then. Ian's champagne funeral had taken place only two months before. Dad seemed to be anticipating something new and wonderful. I do believe he was ready – he felt that his work here on earth was done for this time around.

The next day I was sitting beside Dad's hospital bed when my mobile phone rang. Vowing that I would never feel cut off from communication again, I had bought one for myself and each child immediately after that fateful night when I could not find a phone box to get information about the Chinook crash. This time it was Niven wanting to speak to the only remaining male family member he felt he could talk to. I watched my gentle dad nod and smile and say, 'Yes, son, I will. OK! Goodbye.'

'What did Niven say?' I asked.

'Oh, he just asked me was I on my way out and I said yes – so he asked me if when I saw his dad I would tell him that he loved him. I said I would.'

I am sure he did. He went a day later: having decided that he was ready, he just lay down to die. My brother-in-law coined the phrase that Len Cheshire caught the eleven o'clock train to heaven just as he would have wished on his next journey.

Just a few months after our dad's death my sister and I were sitting beside Mum's bed in the Sue Ryder hospice when she looked up and said, 'Hello, Len,' then turned to us and asked, 'What's your dad doing there?' We could not see him, but I am certain he had come back for her as he had never liked to travel without her by his side. She died peacefully the next day. They were born in the early years of the twentieth century within six months of each other, and they had the same six-month gap between their departures.

My family and I continued to go to funerals for what seemed an eternity. Getting up each morning, one almost started to wonder where today's funeral would be. My sister commented that it all paled into nothingness in comparison to the loss of Ian – a wonderfully brave and empathetic statement, given that she had lost her two best friends in our parents. It was Pauline who had been there for them in their later years when I was in Ireland, just as they had been there for her when her first marriage broke down. I knew what she meant, and we did seem to succumb to a kind of numbness. I am not sure that I started to grieve for my parents until several years later, such was my mental state. I now know that in the depths of grief we come to know and value life if we can stay sane enough to gain the understanding on the far side of the pain. We continually reassured ourselves that our parents had not suffered for too long and that their passing had been a blessing at the right time for them both. At that time I was just desperately casting about to find an appropriate behavioural response to the muddy swamp of life that seemed to be breeding crocodiles faster than I could fish them out. I think numb is not a bad place to be, and our own brain chemicals eventually sort out the situation by allowing us to feel, scream and float in alternating patterns. I certainly did plenty of crying for many months and I often wondered where all of that fluid came from as I dripped my way through boxes of tissues.

Just to keep us on our toes, my son was involved in a serious car crash just two months after Mum's death. Niven was on his way to study for his final university exams in Coleraine University in the very north of County Antrim. As his little Mini ambled along country lanes bordered by rustic stone walls that keep the sheep on the hilly pastureland, another car chose to overtake an oncoming vehicle on the brow of a hill. Niven had no chance, as the vehicle ploughed straight into him on his own side of the road. What prompted him to squeeze out of a tiny crack in the door and run up the hill before collapsing in the ditch we don't know; he only felt that he must not burn like his dad and his colleagues. It was truly a miracle that he survived such a wreck without any broken bones, although he was badly lacerated and bruised. To this day I feel it was his father who lifted him from the wreckage, and during his recovery Niven wrote a very poignant poem that suggested he too felt the 'hidden help'. It is possible that it was written in a state of delirium induced by anaesthetic but, whatever its origin, it meant a lot to me as I continued to be grateful for those good things that I could still appreciate.

The six months that it took Niven to recover turned into a blessing, because they gave us time to discuss our grief and our changed lives before we moved on to the next step. The children and I arranged a memorial outing on the first anniversary of Ian's death, and chose the Belfast Opera House because he had loved organising theatre trips for his friends. We had intended to invite just a few of them, but in true Phoenix style things got slightly out of hand.

Eventually over fifty friends got wind of the event and asked if they could come along. It was a great tribute to Ian, and to us as a family; the champagne reception also helped to keep up the old tradition. What a wonderful reminder to us of how good people really are; our gratitude, as our *annus horribilis* drew to a close, was boundless.

Many people have since asked me where I found the strength to get up each morning during that first year. I kept telling myself that it was what Ian would have expected. He always had great faith in my abilities. He often said that I was his strength, but in reality I knew that it was the reverse. In those early days and months, getting up in the mornings was difficult. One asks, 'What for?' One asks for a very long time.

9
New Lives – Old Chapters

It concerned me that Niven, Nicola and her partner Bob were obviously worried about me and asked how I felt on a regular basis; they continued to show me intense love and were profoundly concerned about my welfare. But I wanted to remove the burden of a deeply grieving mother from their lives so that they could spread their wings and fly. This was one of the reasons I eventually decided to move to France in 1996; the other was that it seemed to be a handier place to escape prying eyes as I wrote what proved to be a very controversial book about their father's life. The idea of moving and writing came at just the right time to allow some adrenalin to flow back into my pain-filled brain, although other synchronicities contributed to the decision.

One of these had been initiated, unremarked by anyone at the time, when in 1973 I gave birth to our son in Larne maternity hospital. A few days later another boy was born in the same place to a man named Jack Holland, and he and Ian may well have passed each other in the hospital corridors. I can imagine the two men nodding to each other as they passed in those dismal disinfected corridors: 'How're ye doing?' they would have said with true Ulster civility. It would take almost twenty-one years before their paths crossed again.

Ian and I eventually met the Hollands as a result of renting their lovely old apartment in the walls of a church beside a lake in Italy for one of our last holidays. We invited them to our home so that they could vet us to see if we were suitable to rent what was in fact their home in Europe; their real home was in New York, where Jack worked for an Irish news-paper. They had been back in Belfast for a while when we met; we immediately got on well together and, had we not lived in the unreal and bitter world that was Belfast then, we would have developed a warm friendship. Later, we reflected that we would have been just two couples who liked each other and shared a social life if we had not met in Northern Ireland. When we eventually arrived at their lovely Italian home we marvelled at their well-stocked library lining the walls. The views of the lake from their terrace, and sipping a local wine while working our way through this fine array of books, were our idea of heaven. That is, until Ian called me from preparing some culinary masterpiece with his usual eloquence: 'Fuck me! Come and look at this – I don't believe it!' He was holding in his hand the autobiography of a former chief of staff of the IRA. The fact that it was a personally autographed copy added a certain interest to Ian's look of amused incredulity. When he eventually calmed down and stopped chuckling at the bizarre situation of finding himself in the home of an author who seemed to have a decidedly Nationalist viewpoint on the Irish situation, he had another of his bright ideas. 'What a pity I can't tell Jack what I do,' he mused. 'We could certainly write an entertaining book together!'

Sadly, to protect both Jack and Ian we had to distance ourselves from them socially when we returned home. The two men shared a great sense of fun and the ridiculous in life, but keeping conversations restricted to 'safe' topics was not our scene. We tried going out to dinner together a few times, but Ian found it too painful to live a lie and knew that no one would believe that the two men did not know more about each other than they in fact did at that time.

Oddly, Jack Holland had written another book, a historical novel called *The Fire Queen* which I had chosen to read some years before we met because it was based in my home area of East Anglia. The fact that of all the obscure titles that I should pick to read was one written by an Irishman from Belfast who was to be a future writing colleague in those pain-filled days of 1996 is another of life's inexplicable synchronicities.

On the morning of Ian's funeral I had received a phone call from Mary Hudson, Jack's American wife. We had not been in contact with each other for many months, but she had seen a photograph of Ian as it flashed on to the television screen: 'The funeral will take place today out of his home of Detective Superintendent Ian Phoenix . . .' She had been stunned, not knowing whether she was more shocked that he had died or that he had been a policeman.

Jack and Mary often reflected that our friendship was another victim of the Belfast Troubles. I asked Jack to write Ian's story with me because I wanted to achieve balance and tell the story the way Ian would have appreciated it, so inviting a Northern Ireland journalist and novelist who came from a Nationalist background seemed an excellent idea. (I am not so sure that the security services agreed, however.) Although Jack and Mary were now living in New York, his historical knowledge and excellent memory suited my needs – in fact, rather irritatingly, he remembered more dates connected with Ian and me than I do myself. As part of the research we plodded our way through my earlier life – sometimes crying, curiously laughing and often marvelling at the life I had led with Ian. We almost had fun with the writing. I watched Jack fall in love with the character he never had the chance to get to know.

Once the manuscript was handed over to the Defence Advisory Committee for vetting we were hounded by secret service agencies. With the usual government agency efficiency all manner of miscommunication took place. Somewhere along the line it was forgotten that we had been very discreet and secure in our writing and had actually asked for official help with safety issues before it was seen by anyone other than Roland, our editor. In, I now realise, typical 'top-secret' manner large parts of the carefully guarded, secure manuscript were photocopied and handed out to too many police officers and minor civil servants. Really furious and hurt, for the first time in ages, I received an apology from the Chief Constable of the RUC who had not known that upsetting phone calls had been made to my children by an old colleague of Ian's after totally misinterpreting my reasons for writing the book. Or maybe this 'friend' was just slightly miffed not to get his own written first. Shaking off some of my naïvety, I had to learn that jealousy is a powerful motivator.

I had anticipated criticism once the book was published, but it came earlier than that, and from some of the most unexpected quarters. Praise, too, came from astonishing places. It is heartening that even now, eight years after publication, I still receive letters of gratitude for sharing the story with the world. Police officers and ex-prisoners alike have thanked me for being so honest in presenting a real person's story. That, for me, is better than any headstone that I might have erected for Ian. I also see his book as a tribute to all of those men and women across the world who work to keep society safe in the often maligned security services. I could not have known in the years before September 11 that many of Ian's prophecies about negotiating with terrorists would come true. Unfortunately, history has proved him to be a far greater strategist than we could have known at the time.

Perhaps that is also why the British government at the time did not want our book published in its original form, but asked me to cut about one-third of the manuscript. After discussion with Jack I agreed to see government representatives and discuss exactly why some parts were deemed to be unsafe to print. They had a shock, I think, because they probably believed that we would just accede to their demands: I could hear Ian's voice saying, 'Giv'em a run for their money!' After much negotiation and many long, arduous discussions with Special Branch personnel I agreed to remove or adapt approximately one-fifth of the manuscript, provided that they convinced me it would endanger someone's life to leave it as it was. I knew that this was the right moral standpoint, for without Ian to guide me I could not possibly have known what would be dangerous at that time.

It amazed the security services that I did in fact know where to find Ian's diaries, carefully hidden by him in case of his premature death, and that he and I had discussed aspects of his work as intelligent people in an equal and loving relationship. He had always reminded me that, if anything were to happen to him, I should get hold of his records immediately as he felt they had a contribution to make to history. Ian knew that a shredder would await this almost unique record of police work if I did not get there first.

Jack and I chose to write as much as we did because a so-called peace process was in motion at the time of writing, and in our innocence we did not realise that in fact an undercover war was continuing from both sides of the community in Ireland. Nevertheless, despite the fact that we had clearly had access to Ian's own account, a witch-hunt was carried out within the security forces to see if anyone had helped me with the details. Again, in that irritatingly patronising manner employed by government agencies it had been assumed that I as a mere wife would not have had the knowledge of Ian's life and thoughts that I indeed had. How I dislike stereotyping and assuming the obvious rather than looking deeper into a situation – I always try not to make a judgement until all the facts are there. I was upset that the loyal, brave men and women who had worked with Ian were assumed to have helped me with my information, when in fact they had all been only too willing to share their funny stories of Ian for my comfort but none of them had been aware that I was even dreaming of writing such a story. They certainly would not have shared any top-secret information, being the security professionals that they truly were.

Jack and I were sad that we were asked to remove some very funny stories about so-called terrorists and their bizarre behaviour during the Ulster Troubles. When the surprise manuscript was eventually made available to the security services for advice, the reaction of some of Ian's colleagues was mixed but sometimes comical. One senior officer who had worked for Ian, and was asked by the security services to look at the manuscript to help work out what was too dangerous to print, was reported to be 'tutting' his disapproval of my 'betrayal' as he read. 'How could she write such treason?' he demanded. To him it was 'disgusting' and he was convinced that 'Ian Phoenix would *never* have cried at the death of IRA terrorists!' The last comment was a reference to the still controversial deaths of a group of armed killers who had tried to blow up officers in a police station at Loughall. Ian had arrived home visibly upset, although of course relieved that the operation had been successful. His words to me were, 'Why do young Irishmen in the IRA continue to risk their lives attempting to kill their fellow

Irishmen in the police, when they could so easily use their talents to build the country up rather than destroying it all?' The sight of fit young men lying dead as a result of their misguided aims was very upsetting to Ian, and he deplored such a waste of life. The fact that he did not burst into tears in the office did not mean that he did not care, as seemed to be the assumption of the vetting officer. There's that stereotype again – 'Men don't cry.' What a load of rubbish!

This officer continued with his castigation of what he perceived to be my misguided action in writing the book and then suddenly had a great idea of his own: 'By the way, when they make the film I would like to have my role played by Gene Hackman!' Mixed emotions indeed. He would perhaps have been devastated to know that I turned down a film offer – much to Jack Holland's annoyance. I recently discovered the letter that I sent to him from France, on 19 May 1997, after he had been approached by a famous producer to turn our book into a movie. My raw emotion is still evident:

Dear Jack

I realise that I owe you an explanation for what may appear a turn-around in my decision-making processes. I have been in quite a deep depression for several weeks now and I have had to spend a lot of time alone recently to try and sort myself out.

The rest of the letter goes on to explain that I could not possibly conceive of writing a screenplay about Ian's life and death when just trying to write up a graphic scene had given me terrible physical pain, and I felt there was no possibility in continuing with something now that I could no longer remain objective about it. I felt that I had done my job for Ian's memory with the book, and now it was time to put myself back together. The final sentences reflect this 'nothingness' that made me so sad and bereft all over again:

> I feel so restless I am in danger of bursting. I have decided to go back to Ireland next week to see if I can sort out my feelings there. . . .
>
> Anyway dear Jack, I will stop now. I shall be back here to receive you and Mary later in the summer and I look forward to that. We can drink good wine and eat in the sunshine whilst I peruse a future of God knows what.
>
> Love to Mary and keep up the good work.
>
> Susan

This reminds me only too well of how I felt at that lowest spot in my life: later that month the Irish Sea looked very inviting indeed, and not for sailing on. What had been a literary project for Jack had been, of course, my life, and although I had used the writing as a cathartic process I had somehow managed also to make it a way of absenting myself from my own life – I had taken a step back in order to report on myself in a very objective manner. In the increasingly popular neuro-linguistic programming courses (NLP) this kind of behaviour, where one steps off one's own timeline for self-protection, is treated or reprogrammed very effectively. Unfortunately, at that time I neither knew nor cared about any such therapies.

Some sad people did in fact suggest that by writing the book I was only cashing in on the publicity of the Chinook crash. My answer is that, no matter how Ian had died, I would have written his story, because he had wanted to do this himself in retirement and several other writers of the time were including him in their books. I wanted to make sure that his story came from me. Perhaps, had I waited until I was feeling more balanced, I would have written it differently; we will never know. It was my catharsis. Nevertheless I am happy that Ian's final bit of boat-rocking was in fact published and became a bestseller.

When the nine months of writing and cross-Atlantic faxing, and a further six months of adrenalin-filled M15 meetings, publicity and press dates, had finished I went down a very deep hole. Some cheeky people suggested that it was prompted by appearing on the *Richard & Judy* morning TV programme, but I found their interview exceptionally sensitive and genuinely caring. When I look back now, I wonder how I did it without bursting into tears. I think I was in some odd way still doing Ian's work. It was his message that I wanted to get across, an important message that he wanted to convey to people in power about dealing with terrorists. The fact that it also dealt with our personal life and gave many people an insight into the lives of a policeman's family proved to be very popular. In fact most of the press interviews were very sympathetic, and people were genuinely interested in hearing a story that for once supported the law-and-order side of life. The media wanted to know that real people were involved in keeping society safe – real people with real feelings and families who loved them. Many said that it made a pleasant change from the stereotypical policemen and their families portrayed in television dramas. It seemed to be refreshing for people to see wives who support their husband's chosen career and don't continually run home to Mum, drink themselves under the table or have an affair when the going gets tough. But suddenly my last job for Ian was complete, the publicity was over and I had to think about me and what I would do with the rest of my life.

A bleak, empty, devastated space was sitting where my heart should be.

It was 1997. I should have been pulling myself together by now, according to popular theory. I had lost my husband and both parents, but three years had passed of which I really cannot remember many events from the first two. I do remember buying my first house in the Lot-et-Garonne region of south-west France. It had been January 1996 when Nicola and I found the little stone-built property on the corner of a country road, with wisteria branches in their winter sleep rambling from ground to roof. 'It's a bit above your budget,' said John the *immobilier*, in true estate agent-speak. Unfortunately, by the time he was saying that we were in the kitchen cooing over how great it would be to cook for friends there. It was perfect for the single entertainer, as the dining area was just across the rustic serving island in clear view of the cooking area. I could already envisage the guests chatting with me and drinking their aperitifs as I prepared supper. So the deal was done and I bought my first property as a single woman near the little town of Eymet.

John had sold me much more than a house – more like a lifestyle in France. He and his wife Chrissy also turned out to be my long-suffering neighbours. It was such a comfort when I had first arrived in France to know that I had neighbours, just five minutes down the road, who knew the ropes. I often think that the shy and gentle Chrissy must have been an angel in disguise to put up with my visits in those early days. Her husband sold me the perfect house in which to recuperate, and loaned his patient and caring wife to listen to my chatter when I needed to unload. They took me to many of their social occasions when I still knew no one in the area: 'We have this new neighbour – would you mind if she came along?' I also went with them to the local cricket club –

Eymet has a real English cricket club, which welcomes all newcomers to the region. Here I must be honest and say that I always thought cricket was as exciting as watching paint dry, but I was truly pleased to be invited to join the friendly group who supported the players. My passport was a bottle of Belfast gin. In those days one could buy a pretty bottle suitable for a gift with a painting of the *Titanic* on the label – no, I won't do any 'sinking feeling' gin jokes here. Chrissy and I drove in one Sunday afternoon to join the ladies who were making sandwiches for the players, I produced my bottle as a 'hello' present and was welcomed with warm smiles.

It was in that first stone cottage that I licked my wounds, wrote Ian's life story and learned to love the rural French people and their culture. I had initially thought that I would move between Ireland and France, spending six months in each country, but I could find only pain back in Ireland and wondered why I was suffering for nothing. Someone suggested that I was running away from my life, but when I thought about that comment I realised that I could see nothing to run from or to. I was my life now; Ireland had been my life with Ian. I no longer needed those roots, any more than I needed the roots of my childhood home. I have never felt the need to be 'rooted' anywhere since I was very young – as long as I have contact with friends and family from time to time I can survive. The children would come to me no matter where I chose to live. Home is where the heart is, but my heart was having a lot of problems deciding where it wanted to be.

Back I went to my house in Ireland with a view to renting it out. Nicola and her husband Bob came to the rescue by deciding to spend a year there and put some TLC back into the poor old 'Acre' overlooking the Irish Sea in County

Antrim, and I started to prepare for my departure. It was a much harder step than I had anticipated and I invented excuses for almost three months before I finally plucked up the courage to leave. It was another 'first' to do alone, though a little more daunting than the cinema outing in Dublin. The amount of possessions I decided to cram into the car with me proved a physical challenge in itself. The morning I left, my good friends Jim and Sharon came to help. Jim was going purple, shoving a large cushion in behind my driving seat as he gave me last-minute words of caution: 'Remember, lass, you can't use your rear-view mirror. You'd better make sure to use the wing mirrors on those French autoroutes,' he counselled me in his kindly Cumbrian accent, never lost in spite of being married to an Irishwoman.

As I drove away I saw the sadness and the very genuine love and kindness in the eyes of these two good people who had been our family friends for many years. I left many more friends behind as I drove south. Yes, it was hard, but I knew that I did not want to live my life through the good will of other people for ever. I had my own path to make, though that did not mean that I felt any less love or gratitude for all those good friends that I was moving away from. It is not always possible to keep in regular touch with each individual, but with real friendship it does not matter.

On my two-day journey from Northern Ireland to what was to become my new home in France I was not sure I was making a good decision. But when I was almost there, just north of Angoulême I suddenly felt all right again. I took a deep breath and had a peculiar sense of coming home. There are odd moments in life when one feels that it is OK, and this was one of them. I was later to discover that there may be past-life reasons for these inherent feelings, but for now I was just happy to start feeling excited again.

Slowly I managed to improve my schoolgirl French to a level where I could talk to the neighbours. It was just as well, really, because that first set of neighbours really did find me very strange. They would continually ask me if I did not like my family, and could not understand why I had chosen to move so far away and live alone. Nor could they understand that I could manage without a man in the house. They were convinced that I must have a secret lover tucked away in a cupboard. Anyone who came to call was carefully scrutinised from behind the hedge just in case they had missed a rampant love affair somewhere along the way. I'm afraid they were seriously disappointed.

I roamed the local lanes on my bicycle with a baguette stuck in the basket, trying to blend in. But I never ate the bread – just used it to look ethnic! And I cooked with loads of garlic, making sure that the doors and windows were open, just to let the locals know that the British eat more than bacon, eggs and jam – a genuine shock to many of my French friends.

Every route from the Lot-et-Garonne to the ports of the Channel coast was soon familiar to me. My idea of a road trip took at least eight hours and the passenger seat was full of road maps, water bottles and snacks. I would book overnight ferries whenever possible – either to England or direct to Southern Ireland. This proved to be the easiest way for me, as I knew the car was safe while I slept – sensible, because the boot was usually stuffed with cases of local wine that I thought it my patriotic duty to share with all and sundry. Was I lonely? The answer is no. I have found that being alone does not have to mean lonely. There is a great deal of truth in the idea of being alone in a crowd. I always found that when travelling alone one is more likely to strike up a conversation with new people. Not that one needs to become bosom buddies, but who was it said that a stranger is only the friend you haven't met yet? Nevertheless, single ladies can be considered a threat to couples if they strike up a conversation with husbands of insecure wives! It took me a while to realise this in my single travels. Ian and I had always included everyone in our conversations, and I just could not understand why anyone should think I wanted to steal their husband or partner in a friendly conversation on a plane or cross-Channel ferry. I do not expect lifelong friendship to result from a casual chat with strangers, but it is amazing just how many interesting people are out there. If we always stick with our own group or partners we miss opportunities to hear other opinions and learn of often outrageously different lifestyles. The world is not so much hazardous as fascinating.

It felt less so one day when I found myself smiling *en passant* at a cool-looking lady as we came face-to-face in a corridor somewhere.

'Do I know you?' she sneered.

'Er, no, I don't think so,' I replied.

Whereupon she flicked her hair, scowled and said, 'Well!' as she flounced on her way.

Whatever the response, I continue to smile at the world and be friendly, otherwise I am not being true to myself. When I have travelled alone in strange environments it has been the acknowledgements from strangers that can make life seem worth while. When we utter a friendly greeting to a stranger, it could well be the only human contact that person has had all day. For true mental health, we need to know that we have been acknowledged in our lives, in however small a way. Acknowledging others is the best way to be greeted back, since we are a mirror to our own world. I recently heard two people describing each other, independently, and these two charming women had both labelled the other as 'cold and frosty'. I wonder which one was cold and frosty first?

However, in spite of all my good intentions I still ended up after a year in my new French life feeling very depressed indeed. I have heard manic-depressives talk about the 'black dog' that comes over their head when times are bad. I can only say that it felt like ten black dogs and all their stray puppies pushing me into a dark tube. I would be talking to a neighbour in France and suddenly burst into tears. '*Oh, la, la,*' she would say, '*la vie c'est dure.*' I would take a drive along the sleepy lanes of Lot-et-Garonne and consider whether I could run into a tree and end it all. As I locked my house doors and quietly screamed the old stone walls down I would wonder what had happened to me. I had tried to find a whole new me as opposed to feeling like half of 'us'. This was me, the always optimistic Susan, who had coped with death and destruction on a big scale. I had looked on the three faces of my dear and departed in a short time; I had viewed, without flinching, photographs of the awful Chinook wreckage and surrounding body pieces that now seemed to reflect the state of my own psyche; I had written and published a controversial book, and spoken to radio and television reporters all over the world. Surely I was stronger than this. I had come such a long way, I thought. Not far enough, obviously.

10
Angels and Energy United

Now the controversy and excitement were over, the children were moving stoically forward and I was physically in France – but where was I mentally, psychologically and spiritually? I was down a black tube, with no possible end in sight and just that potential forty years of blackness ahead that had been so innocently pinpointed by my solicitor. Being torn from loved ones and a comfortable lifestyle causes adrenalin to race through our blood and brain. When we remember, too, that human DNA vibrates at a rate of 52–78 gigahertz a second (in layman's language, very fast indeed!) it is no wonder our body systems end up in a mess at such times. Our basic life energy moves around our bodies and our surrounding energy field in an as yet immeasurable frequency (although we can capture energy from our auric field in Kirlian photography). In later years, I became so fascinated by this energy flow that I purchased a camera capable of recording the colours of the aura in the electro-magnetic field around the body. I knew nothing of this at the time, but I did know that when the naturally balanced flow of this life energy gets blocked, for any number of reasons, we become sick. And so, not surprisingly at this time, I became physically ill.

I have no doubt that our mental state radically alters the frequencies at which our individual cells vibrate to the tune of our inherent energy system. In other words, if we get depressed or suffer any emotional trauma our batteries get knocked off course and need to be not only recharged but realigned. Traditional Chinese medicine has successfully used acupuncture and acupressure for many thousands of years for realigning and unblocking the body's energy systems. Indian Ayurvedic massage works on the same body energies. The list of ancient therapies now being rediscovered would fill another book.

But I did not know any of this at the time; all I knew was that I was having one throat infection after another, and coughing like a sixty-a-day smoker. My shoulders had stiffened and one ankle refused to move on really bad days. I was almost permanently sick. So what does one do when one is ill? I went back to my old doctor in Ireland. I can see him now, looking at me with such compassion.

'Now, Susan, I know you don't like tranquillisers but there's this wonderful antidepressant and after a wee ten-day course you'll feel on top of the world!'

My brain was screaming, 'No, don't do it!' Through the tears and the hacking cough I heard myself saying, 'No, thank you. I've got this far without drugs, so there must be another way.' But my other self was shouting, 'Fool! Take the tablets – get a quick fix. Go on – why not do it?'

I walked out of his surgery sobbing, hoping no one had noticed me. A day later I found myself on the treatment couch of Mandy, an old friend from university days who had made contact shortly after Ian's death. I well remember the slightly hesitant voice on the phone: 'Susan, I feel so useless in the face of your grief, but wonder if I could offer a little something that may help.' Mandy is a bold and beautiful personality who had changed track and at the time of her phone call was studying aromatherapy and reflexology. She offered me an hour of aromatherapy massage 'to help you relax'. I was at the stage when if someone had asked me to jump off a high building with a kite I would have tried it. Of course I accepted the gracious offer, and she even managed to make me feel as if I were doing her a favour by helping with her course case studies. What a case study I would turn out to be.

What bliss it was on that first visit to feel the all-encompassing warmth and sweet-smelling energy in Mandy's treatment room – such pure, sweet relaxation. How comforting were her kind, strong face and the feeling of peace I had. Yes, I could manage my pain. I would learn how to use these beautiful oils for myself. Each essential oil has its own special quality in this, nature's own healing power – long neglected in the name of science. How good it would be to smell lavender oil and frankincense in a hospital ward or doctor's surgery, where relaxation is crucial to the healing process. Mandy actually managed to make me giggle when telling me which oils made one feel sexy, and I pretended I could imagine a new life ahead when I would use such wonderful aids. Sex being the furthest thing from my mind, I actually concentrated on those which I would choose to burn in my house to keep my emotions in balance. Back home afterwards, I lit little candle burners and bought electrical heat stones and discs for the light bulbs to make sure my olfactory senses could get their 'fix' whenever I needed one.

I often reflect on why, when science became a gift to medicine, the old healing tools in nature were neglected: the baby was mostly thrown out with the bathwater. I was equally guilty, in my early twenties, with all of my young person's vigour and limited knowledge. As my dad used to say, 'A little knowledge is a dangerous thing!' I had studied physiology since the age of twelve when I first joined the St John's Ambulance voluntary first aid corps. I had known then that I needed to serve the community in some way. I loved learning about medical and scientific discoveries.

When as a child I read that William Withering had discovered the heart drug digitalis in 1775 in foxgloves, I marvelled at the bounty to be found in the hedgerows. Years later Ian, too, was to make herbal teas from wild flowers and garden produce. When I look back, we obviously both had an inherent interest in healing potions and naturopathy. But it was not until we were mature adults that we went down this route. My recent research, forty years on from childhood, revealed that Withering did not actually make the discovery himself, and could not personally help a seriously ill patient with his eighteenth-century version of medicine. The patient only managed to recover by visiting a gypsy healer in the countryside. When Withering set off to ask this wise woman what she had used, it was the humble foxglove that proved to be the significant ingredient. Medicine recorded the discovery for scientific acclaim, but what happened to the gifted rural healer whose knowledge was purloined?

When I first arrived as a young bride in Ireland, I heard my mother-in-law talk of 'cures' in the local community and scoffed. Oh, for hindsight and an older head on those stroppy young shoulders! There was so much to learn, and I thought I knew it all at twenty. Learning is not the same as study or training, but bigger than both. Nor is it just finding out what others already know, as in university education. Learning requires a dynamic energy force from within the individual that continues to be curious and adventurous throughout life. In fact, an exciting and interesting eighty-one-year-old lady told me recently that it is curiosity that keeps her young and healthy. Resting on one's laurels is indeed a very green and slippery place to stand.

Green, rural Ireland had maintained its faith in so many of the old folklorish ways. I, as a young English nurse, closed my mind to this. If only I had stopped to do some research: I now know that those gifted people must have been very special and could so easily have worked in tandem with local medics. Twenty-five years later, newly widowed, I was about to be convinced by Mandy and her life-giving aromatherapy. I began to go regularly for a fragrant, relaxing massage and eventually for reflexology, which proved extremely helpful in monitoring my mental and physiological state.

Reflexology is on one level a foot massage which is used to stimulate some of the seventy thousand nerve endings on the soles of the feet. This in turn, it is claimed, helps to clear a system of energy zones or channels in the body corresponding to body organs, similar to the lines of meridian used by acupuncturists and other complementary therapists. It has been reported since ancient Egyptian times that applying pressure to areas of the feet can help a whole host of ailments in the related body parts.

As Mandy worked expertly around the soles of my feet I became very sensitive to the corresponding responses. We began to know me quite well, and indeed enjoyed monitoring my progress back to happiness and wholeness. The laughter that we shared made me realise one day that I had learned a whole new repertoire of vocabulary.

At the end of one reflexology session Mandy casually asked, 'Would you like me to balance your chakras?'

'Yes, please,' I replied, equally casually, before spluttering with laughter.

'What?' she asked in astonishment through her own giggles.

'Listen to us,' I said. 'We sound like a pair of old hippies – us, the scientifically educated graduates from the University of Ulster!' Chakra balancing, indeed – I wondered what Ian would have thought of my new vocabulary. I would find out later.

But all that had taken place three years earlier, and now I wanted to run away to anywhere that would remove the pain of grief, which had returned with a vengeance. Suddenly, there I was in 1997 disappearing down the black tube with the family of black dogs in my head. I arrived for my reflexology session in tears, as I so often did when I met kind people. Confrontation with government ministers and those who were opposed to the fight for widow's rights I could cope with, but kindness and sympathy reduced me to a sobbing mess.

Mandy worked hard on my feet for an hour that day, and I could feel my desperation reflected in her hands on my feet. Where once she had pressed my big toe and I had seen beautiful blues and purples starting to swirl through the black on my retina, I now saw just black – and to the core of my soul. How I longed for those days when Mandy had teased me that she would know whenever I had found another partner because it would be evident on one of my toes. Even though I had thought men were the last thing on my mind then, I realised I was in a much worse state now as I searched again for a positive meaning to my life, a reason to get up in the morning. We both did our best to cheer my spirit and we hugged goodbye as I left, trying to pretend that I was feeling better than when I arrived. As I drove away from Mandy's treatment room the sea in Belfast Lough looked grey and choppy – an almost perfect reflection of my inner self.

Weeks later Mandy told me that as she went back into her treatment room a most dreadful smell met her. No, it was not me – I had showered that day; she could only describe it as the smell of death. She had to get rid of the tape of normally relaxing and beautiful music she had played during the session, and the room's energy needed to be completely changed and cleansed with burning joss sticks and refreshing oils. This was something else I would learn to do in my own environment later, but that day Mandy had to work hard to clean and raise the energy in her treatment room after I had truly lowered the vibrations.

My energy was completely knocked askew, although I was not really aware of this at the time. I was waiting for the right person to enter my life and say something that made sense. What I didn't want to hear were those well-meant platitudes such as, 'Well, you're not getting any younger, you know. You'll be happier when you have grandchildren to look after', or, 'Once you can pull yourself together, you'll be fine.' The worst one, I found, was, 'Time will help', although of course it is true. I remember thinking, despite my children and good friends, that with any luck it would be an awful terminal illness and I could follow Ian. I could almost hear him talking to me: 'Can't I go anywhere on my own?'

Before I left Mandy had told me that my aching joints could be a focus for some treatment, and had given me the business card of a man called Ivan who was an osteopath in Lisburn, County Antrim. Normally osteopaths don't tackle psychological cases, but I had all these obscure physical aches and pains as one does when in mental pain. Any doctor's surgery is full of sad and lonely people who are suffering physical ailments that are really caused by mental anguish of some form or another. We have all been there. The pain is a physical representation of another, deeper problem. 'Psychosomatic' is an unkind word – that pain is a real phenomenon.

I was that sick person who was looking for something other than a quick fix. I wanted to know why I felt so physically dreadful, and how to get out of this hole. So Ivan, who proved to be an excellent osteopath, rotated whatever limb I presented and went through his professional repertoire before, wisely, asking me about my life. In due course he nodded knowingly and said, 'I feel that my wife, who practises in the office next door, may be better able to help you than me.' Eureka! A new door was opened and I met someone who knew exactly what was wrong with me. Vivienne, who was a kinesiologist (a practitioner of another complementary therapy that works with meridians and more), knew my problem: I was ill with soul pain. My deepest inner self and soul were screaming for help and nourishment. There does not seem to be a way for a damaged soul to exhibit itself in modern society, so when it wants to scream 'Help!' it is our physical body that has to express this situation. If you think about this for a moment you will probably recall moments in your life when you suffered a sore throat because there were things you wanted to say to a loved one (or a not so loved one) but were holding back none the less. Or perhaps a stiff knee or back suddenly disappeared when you found a way forward in your personal or professional life. They are all blockages in our energy systems or our soul patterns, depending on how you like to think about it. Even negative energy directed at you from some unfriendly person can cause, say, back or shoulder pain. Our own energy surrounding the body can interact with that of another person, without our conscious knowledge. The expression 'back-stabbing' does not just refer to a mental anguish coming your way.

I lay on Vivienne's couch as she tested my body's energy circuits (meridians) for weakness and blockages. I was clutching a piece of rose quartz to my solar plexus (just under the ribcage) and cried for what seemed like a very long time. Someone had finally understood my pain, and through kinesiological investigation of my bodily needs had opened the flood gates to release powerful emotion. It seemed a bit ridiculous at the time, when viewed from my 'sensible Susan' perspective. There I was, clutching a chunk of pink rock as if it were my long-lost teddy bear, and crying. I was visualising an old dislike of a dead granny, too – I seem to remember letting this internalised dislike of my granny blow out of the window. That's the way it was, and it was wonderful. Give me rose quartz and visualisation over Prozac any day.

After Mandy, this was the first visit I made to what scientific types like to call an alternative therapist. I prefer to use the term complementary therapist, as in these more enlightened days their services are often used to complement those of the accredited medical professions. Vivienne was an intelligent, well-educated woman who had been trained to a high level in the nursing profession. She knew about and understood physiology (that always helps in this area); and, what's more, she cared about people (and that most definitely helps, but is not always evident, in the so-called caring professions). I have since returned to visit both Mandy and Vivienne, and I am delighted to report that Mandy is being used as a consultant by the health service and Vivienne receives many referrals for her therapies. There is a God after all.

Back to synchronicity again – I know, I like the word; you can call it timing or even coincidence if you prefer. After I had experienced that great feeling of release and had been given a herbal potion to drink Vivienne told me she was going to something called a Diana Cooper angel workshop in Exeter in a few days' time, and suggested it might be of interest to me too. I took the leaflet as I left, but had no intention of going on any angel courses. I was now feeling considerably better – and anyway, I was going home to France, wasn't I?

Wrong again. Synchronicity took over after a telephone chat with my son-in-law, Bob, as I travelled south: he pointed out that I had never been averse to changing my mind in the past, so why didn't I just turn round and go on the course? So it was that I found myself in Exeter with a group of other people, many of whom did not know why they were there either. We were eighteen students and Diana Cooper, the angel lady, as many people call her. What a surprise! Not a white fluffy wing in sight. No angelic self-satisfied smiles, or even much of a warm welcome actually; just a group of individuals all asking what exactly it meant to be on a course called Ascension Week. I had half supposed, too, that the participants would be a bunch of middle-aged women with nothing else to do, but actually they comprised quite a cross-section of society including professional people, and spanned an age group, males and females, from twenties to fifties. No obvious silver-haired purple rinses, poodles, hippies or ladies who lunch! OK, so there may have been a few hippies and ladies who lunch but I suppose I am probably a bit of both of those now. No, I am not into headbands and beads – yet.

When I arrived at the retreat centre feeling very uncertain and more than a little scared, I really had no idea that I would rediscover an essence of Ian or see master spirits from another dimension. If I had, I might well have gone home right then. Luckily for me I stayed, and proceeded to make friends with some really interesting and life-changing people.

The other seventeen all seemed to have very little in common with each other, although I felt that they all had some relation to earlier times in my life. By this I mean that they represented areas that I had known and loved over my previous forty-six years, such as East Anglia, Ireland and Scotland. Many of us felt that we had met before but did not know where; it may sound far-fetched, but that is the way it felt. I even shared a room with someone who lived in a part of England very close to where I had grown up. We shared a room reluctantly – neither of us had wanted to give up our privacy – but it worked out well for us both, because we were able to share notes about each day's weird and wonderful discoveries. It took a while for us to discover and acknowledge what exactly we were doing there at all. We had, it appeared, both arrived almost by accident as a result of other people's last-minute cancellations, and our only previous knowledge of angels was limited to Christmas cards and religious imagery. I had always loved the stained-glass windows in medieval churches, and their beautiful depictions of angels had been a favourite of mine since childhood; but I can't say that I had ever paid much attention to their meaning or different forms since they always seemed to belong more to the cultural world inhabited by my Roman Catholic friends. On that first evening my room-mate and I discussed what we thought all this would have to do with us as we learned about the concept of ascension. Would we fly, or go to heaven, or just float about the ceiling a lot? We laughed almost hysterically in our rather grotty little room as we fantasised about the week to come.

But on the first day when we actually sat down with Diana in a big circle, I suddenly felt that this was OK. Group work I understood from my days in therapy and counselling with deaf people and their families. Once again I had the feeling that I had been with all these people somewhere before: very strange, I thought. It seemed even stranger when Diana started to tell us about the special energies that were now being sent to earth to help bring about world peace for the new millennium. She mentioned Ascended Masters. What were they? I didn't know, but as she spoke I could see a number of human-like shapes moving into the room behind her. I can see them now in my mind's eye – Darth Vader types in greyish shadow standing together at the back of the room. I blinked and they were still there, with large flattish shoulders and long flowing cloaks. I decided that I was more depressed than I had realised: I was definitely cracking up! Later I asked Ann, a clairvoyant lady from Southern Ireland, if she had seen anything in the room during the group work. She described exactly what I had seen in detail. She even gave them the name that Diana had mentioned: the Ascended Masters. I wasn't sure whether to be happy that I was not cracking up after all, or really scared. In the end I decided it felt fine, and began to listen to what Ann was saying.

'Would you like a healing?' she was asking.

'I'm not sure. What is it?' I asked in my ignorance. I had heard of healers, of course, but had no idea what they did. I thought it was something to do with churches and hospitals, but really had not given it much thought in spite of my early research into complementary therapies.

'Trust me,' she continued. 'I think there's a reason why I've just approached you, and I've seen a very nice peaceful room for meditation and healing here in the grounds. Shall we try it?'

Why not? I felt I had nothing to lose, and even though I had never met this very kind and obviously wise lady before this week it seemed a good idea to trust her. Soon I was receiving my first healing session, relaxing on a treatment couch and putting myself completely in Ann's hands as she trotted about the room with a brass bowl which, as she struck it with a wooden baton, made very pleasant gonging sounds. In fact I now know she was feeling the vibrational energy in the room and creating her own peaceful haven within that energy. I now also know that a highly attuned healer or psychic person can sense the energy from several different dimensions. Scientists have started to identify such dimensions and call it String Theory. But at the time, all I knew was that it felt very soothing and I closed my eyes to let her get on with whatever she chose to do as I sensed something like an electrical field around my whole body. I was not sure if I wanted to cry the kind of tears that just seep out when you are relaxed, or smile benignly. In fact, as soon as I stopped thinking about it I probably did both. Once the unconscious is allowed to take over from the conscious mind a blissful state is much more easily achieved – not a gin and tonic in sight, and I felt I was floating nicely. Our lives are so full of striving and surviving that it is easy to forget that only around 5 per cent of our cognitive consciousness is in action at any one time.

Those hidden depths that modern literature likes to talk about so glibly are indeed buried deep within each of us. I often advise friends who are deeply stressed to stop thinking and just *be* for a few minutes – stop thinking, start feeling. It is not easy to do, but switching off those thoughts about the price of petrol, the mortgage, future plans or whatever occupies your waking moments is a very important step towards finding out what else is going on in your head and heart and soul. Before you say, 'But I know myself better than anyone else!' stop and ask yourself if you really know what is causing that recurring itch, nightmare, little niggling anxiety or the fact that you have kept banging your toe recently – oh yes, and your cellphone isn't working. Of course you do: you will already be thinking about it with that limited 5 per cent of your brain instead of just letting go and seeing what comes up from the deeper recesses. That answer from deep down may be a surprise to you. The Universe is continually giving us signs that we can still surprise ourselves – an exciting situation, like rediscovering a long-lost love.

The deeper parts of our own minds can be fascinating. One of the tenets of Christianity is that we should love our neighbour as ourselves. In reality that may not be such a great deal, because many of us don't love ourselves at all and we certainly don't spend as much time getting to know ourselves as we do the hunk who lives down the road or the blonde who works in the local pub.

These thoughts will be developed in later chapters. For now let's get back to me, on the couch in a treatment room with the Irish clairvoyant who was making my aura tingle without even touching me. 'Aura' was another word that I learned that week. The dictionary definition is interesting here: Collins 5th edition (2000) tells us that in parapsychology aura means 'an invisible emanation produced by and surrounding a person or object: alleged to be discernible by individuals of supernormal sensibility'. It is interesting because, although I already knew about the energy fields that surround and inhabit living things, on that course I discovered that we can indeed learn to see such energy fields; we do not have to be 'supernormal' beings but just need to relax and believe what we see. It seems odd to me that we watch hours of television or film and accept as fact so many strange phenomena from that somewhat unreal medium, yet when we see a light glow around a person or tree at twilight, when it is easier to recognise, we discount it. Try it. Sit quietly, preferably at twilight, in the garden or anywhere out of doors, and look slightly to the side of a tree or a person. I find that it helps at first to squint slightly and almost defocus on the edge of the person's head or the crown of the tree against the sky. You will eventually see a light aura or halo effect around the edge. That is what we connect with when we hold our hands near to a person's body without physically touching them. That is what I felt initially as I lay with my eyes closed, waiting to see what kind of healing Ann would bring to me. I think we were both surprised at what she did deliver.

'I have someone beside me who wants to communicate with you,' she said.

My eyes flew open: who was it? I couldn't see anyone, but I could definitely discern a change in the energy around us both. I knew I had to trust her, so closed my eyes again just to feel this different energy in the room. It was somehow softer, and I could get the smell of some kind of plant or flower.

Ann was continuing to talk in a soothing voice and making me feel very safe. 'He says, "You didn't have to let him go so soon,"' she continued. 'He says he's still there for you when you need him.'

Of course, who else could it be but Ian? The Ian I had indeed let go very quickly after his death. I had decided that he came back that night after the crash to say goodbye and to tell me, as was his habit when alive, to 'get on with life'. He had often said that looking back was a waste of time and that we should only ever look forward as we progressed in life. Only in his later years did he look back and wave or blow a kiss as he left me to go to work. The day he walked away for ever he had not looked back, but I had gazed a little longer at his departing back for some unknown reason. His military terminology was much in evidence; for instance, at times of stress he would say, 'Just keep low and keep moving.' I believed he would have expected me to have the strength to cope with all that came my way and to do so without help. It was just that I had not kept low (certainly not with a controversial book about his life), although I had kept moving – into a new life in France. Now I was being told I could get a little help from another dimension that I had only previously glimpsed on very few occasions in my life.

Ann told me she could feel an almost overwhelming

sensation of love all around her and that she was enjoying the feeling. Now here was the spirit of my soulmate – back for two seconds and already chatting up another woman! I couldn't have cared less, but felt elevated as this complete stranger continued to tell me what he was saying to her, relaying things that she could not possibly have known without knowing our lives. He talked, for instance, of our children and my depression. Ann also asked me if I wanted to see him – what a question! Of course the answer was yes. She told me that she could see clouds drifting, and if I could just take my subconscious up into these same clouds I would be able to see. I so much wanted to do so, but it was no good – I could not see him. I could imagine his face if I wanted to kid myself, but that was not the point. Yet the beautiful feeling of peace and happiness that had entered the room was enough. I could also smell magnolia blossom, which was a good thing to smell, Ian told Ann. Suddenly I realised that the next house I was trying to buy in France had a magnificent old magnolia tree in the garden. Was he trying to tell me that this was a good move? I only know that I floated out of that room on cloud nine. After his death I had pushed his soul away too quickly. He was there for me when I needed him, and I could talk to him again when at my lowest ebb.

In the previous few years I had tried so hard to move away from what I considered a morbid hanging on to the past. I really did believe that I had laid my ghosts, and did not need to sit and weep on graves in the stereotypical way that widows are supposed to. Perhaps I had tried too hard. I had thought that going over all the old ground with the earlier book had sorted out my need for Ian, but I was wrong. I might have analysed our life together, but what I had neglected was me. That was what he wanted to tell me. I still needed to find myself, the inner person who was an important contributor to this world. In my bid to write the perfect tribute to him I had forgotten who *I* was. It all sounds so very 1960s' America, doesn't it? Now I needed to make a bid to find my inner self. This is what most spiritual journeys are all about, and many so-called psychological needs are in fact spiritual needs. 'Spiritual' is the kind of word that gets hijacked by fanatics, but one of its dictionary definitions is 'relating to the spirit or the soul and not to physical nature or matter; intangible'; another dictionary definition is 'standing in a relationship based on communication between the souls and minds of the persons involved'. These definitions I like very much – let's defend our right to our own personal communication with our own souls and any other good souls that happen to be in this world or another, if that is what brings comfort and growth.

Some religious leaders do not like to admit that perhaps each of us has the power to communicate without their help, and if we are also communicating with spirits and energies in other dimensions we really threaten their power as they want to be the sole conduits to heaven. Too many people have been turned off their journey of self-discovery by just such clerics and self-appointed leaders of religious groups. I believe in a divine source that lights our Universe, and I know that we can access this light when we need to: we just have to give ourselves the time to recognise it.

Which brings me neatly back to the angels as beings of another realm in our Universe. Angels and the concept of ascension were the focus of the course I was attending in Exeter. Ascension, I learned, means raising our vibration to the level of light – back to the vibrating DNA and energy lines again. There are many spiritual leaders from different religious backgrounds in countries worldwide who have been following this philosophy for thousands of years.

Today, Deepak Chopra, Doreen Virtue, Barbara Brennan, William Bloom, Diana Cooper and Carolyn Myss are just a few of the talented, well-educated people from a variety of professional backgrounds who advocate ascension techniques in the form of meditation and mind-body-soul work that allow the individual to chart his or her own path to psychological and spiritual peace and joy. Now before you start to think about the Salvation Army when you read that word 'joy', just ask yourself when you last felt real personal joy – when you on your own felt joy in your life. It takes work and time with yourself to learn that you are worth being with – those TV adverts in which beautiful people tell themselves they can have some luxury product or other 'because I'm worth it' are not so far-fetched as we may think. What are you worth? Certainly you must be worth getting to know more about and honouring yourself. We often throw so much away that we could be using for ourselves: unconditional love starts at home. I recently read a newspaper interview with Lulu the popular singer and was amused to see that each time she mentioned her personal journey of self-discovery, the scathing columnist labelled it as 'claptrap' and 'cliché-ridden rubbish'. It does bring to mind those people who scoffed at the idea of a round rather than a flat world. Is it really claptrap to talk about ourselves and our life progress in spiritual terms? Do we want to know about ourselves and others or not?

That week in Exeter I not only got to know a lot more about myself but also met a few angels on the way. After the experience of the Ascended Masters slipping into the room and then Ian visiting I did not know if I could cope with much more. I learned to meditate for the first time in my life. The most amazing 'trips' were taken each day as Diana gently guided us through the exercises in ascension. We began each morning with yoga specially adapted by Diana to open up the chakras, which are found next to the various hormonal glands and radiate and receive energy. The body's energy system produces hundreds of such points of focus, but most healers and psychics only concentrate on the seven major ones. I had never had so much energy flowing about my sluggish body. As each day progressed the eighteen of us on the course could feel our state changing, so that by the evening we really felt like floating. I kept imagining how much could be saved on drug rehabilitation if all school-children were taught how to do this. I have to admit that I had taken a bottle of my favourite Belfast gin with me just in case anyone fancied a wee aperitif before the tasty vegetarian meal each night. Not only did we not need or feel like drinking alcohol, but I completely forgot about the blue bottle languishing in the boot of my car.

On one of the meditations we were encouraged to do some astral travel outside of our bodies in order to go off and zap love at someone who needed it. In earlier meditations I had been half thinking that I was just indulging in some wonderful dream work. This time, however, proved to be different. On my journey I chose to go to see my daughter Nicola, who I knew was not enjoying her work at that time. As my mind allowed my subconscious to take over I imagined that she was in an office gathering of some kind, and felt myself hovering on the ceiling looking down. It seemed as though I was watching a television screen inside my head – a very odd but real sensation of 'seeing'. My lovely daughter was stand-ing beside her boss and another man whom I didn't recognise, and was holding something in her hand. It was her farewell dinner, I later learned; the scene looked so real that I was very surprised. I did as we were bid and zapped a massive amount of love towards my rather nervous-looking daughter as she stood there receiving a farewell gift from her boss. Then I slowly floated back towards a house in Northern Ireland where I knew that another woman was also having a hard time. This was a friend who had lost her husband at the same time Ian had been killed on the Mull of Kintyre. I saw her sitting crying in a little bed-sitting room she had made for herself at the back of her charming bungalow, and with my mind and love gently tried to encourage her back into the main part of her home where there was more light. The feeling of floating through the atmosphere was truly beautiful, and the whole aura around my body felt light and tingly. My tasks accomplished, I brought myself back into my body and grounded my spirit into the room where the rest of the group were slowly waking up. Looking around at their almost beatific smiles, I knew that everyone was feeling suitably relaxed and equally happy. When the session finished I decided to ring another good friend in Ireland.

'Hello,' is all that I said to Diane when she answered.

'Oh, thank God you're back!'

'No, I'm not. I'm still in England, on a course.'

'I know that – I just mean it's great to hear you sounding normal again.'

I was shocked as this very perceptive and caring friend went on to explain how worried everyone had been about my mental state – I had had no idea that my careful act was not kidding the people who really knew me! You know that weak voice that appears as if from a stranger when you are stressed? She had known from my voice that I had not really been in my body for many months. I had no idea that I had been sounding so pathetic. My soul had been trying to follow Ian, I think.

Diane continued, 'I don't know what it is you're on, but keep taking it – and bring us some back when you're over!'

What I was on, indeed! I was on life and me, I suppose.

The next day I rang my daughter to ask her how she felt and what she had been doing recently. She proceeded to tell me that she had been to an office farewell do, her own in fact, where she had felt particularly emotional and had been asked to make a speech. Apparently she had suddenly recovered herself and had felt a great new energy flow through her which had enabled to her speak with a new self-power; but then she had cried and made a surprisingly un-Nicola-like 'I love you all' goodbye speech, causing everyone else around the table to cry too. Not bad for a bunch of journalists, I reckon. I was, nevertheless, quite shocked as it appeared that I really had travelled to be there with her – just to verify, I asked who the man standing beside her had been. Now it was Nicola's turn to be shocked as she told me who the newcomer to the office was and then asked how on earth I could have known all that as I had not been told her plans for that week. On checking my cellphone I also discovered that my widowed pal in grief had actually tried to ring me at just the time that I was sending her love and encouragement. Spooky or what?

The marvellous experiences continued all week. I saw and felt the presence of angels in many forms and really did feel such comfort that I hardly gave Ian another thought as we went from one beautiful, loving experience to another. Warm and fuzzy ruled supreme. The most traumatic event for me was an exercise where Diana asked us to draw our dreams, and I was immediately hit by that big black dog of depression all over again. I could feel the tears seeping out from under my eyelids as everyone else appeared to be busily drawing glowing dreams for their futures. What was my future? My dreams had all died, and I could not think of one thing in life that I wanted to aim for any more. I kept seeing that beautiful black woman in the film *South Pacific* singing 'You Gotta Have a Dream'. Where had my dreams gone? How could I survive without them?

I do not remember how Diana coped with my tears, but I do still have the really graphic dream picture that I drew later in the week after I had learned so many new skills. I found a new dream. I learned how to use my hands to feel energy fields and auras and to heal gaps in the energy field around a sad person. I was amazed when the person that I was working with told me that she could see the mythological figure of Pegasus when I was gently stroking her aura just a few inches away from her body. I had decided that I would try to give light to her very sad eyes, and was delighted to see them start to shine as she described the Pegasus image that had appeared in her mind's eye. In this way I learned that the winged horse continued to be special to me, and not just as the insignia of the Parachute Regiment. I also learned just how lucky I had been in my life, in spite of my traumatic losses three years earlier, as other group members related their own traumas that had been with them since childhood. It suddenly struck me in one of the group sessions that I was almost the only person there who had had a warm and loving childhood and a happy marriage. Count your blessings time again.

11
Another Step Forward

There I was ready to go back to France and buy my new house with the beautiful magnolia tree in the garden. Before the angel course I had become deeply depressed in the original little cottage in Eymet and had already known that I needed to move on. John, the estate agent, had found me yet another lovely home that answered my needs of the moment. As luck would have it – or another of life's synchronicities – an old friend rang to ask if he could come down for a few days to see what my life in France was like. My first instinct was to say no, as I really wanted to devote some time to the freshly 'angelled' me. On that first angel course I had learned the value of meditation in everyday life. I had lost that sense of being abandoned to get on with life on my own, and I could feel the new sense of peace surrounding me quite tangibly. I now began to feel that there was a distinct purpose to people's lives – similar to the way I had felt as a teenager when I wanted to make a real contribution. I had energy again for the first time in years. In particular I wanted to get on with selling the house and move on to a new path.

Luckily, after some wise words from my son I gave in, since it sounded as though the next visitor needed someone to talk to and old habits die hard. Gary had been a close colleague of Ian's and had often arrived home with him in the old days when he was lonely. In his usual way Ian would say to me, 'Sort him out – help him with the priorities of life.' He had often brought single people home for me to 'counsel' while he filled them with his good wine – I always felt that perhaps the wine was more therapeutic than any words from me. However, Gary and I had become firm friends and he had called me a number of times in previous years to cheer me up when I was feeling down. This happened with others, too, when I was at a low ebb, almost as though they had been prompted to ring me when I needed to be reminded that there are a lot of good people in the world. I am always humbled, and intensely grateful, when I think back to the concern that many of our old friends continued to show to me, through phone calls, letters or a bunch of flowers. I am not so sure that I have always been so attentive and thoughtful to others.

Thus the week that Princess Diana died in Paris found Gary flying down to Bordeaux to see how I was coping with life amongst the vineyards of south-west France. I was happy to have someone to bore or enthuse with my new spiritual ideas, and he in turn was interested to hear about my encounter with Ian's spirit, because Gary and Ian had had great respect for each other. I seem to remember trying to teach Gary to meditate, but he was much more interested in exploring my new environment. He was flattered when some friends asked if he would like to help us pick grapes at their vineyard. It always sounds so romantic, doesn't it? Floating about with a cute basket clipping grapes that will turn into delicious wine to grace our tables. Wrong. It is very hard work – although a lot of fun, with a mixture of French, English and the inevitable Franglais bantered between the rows of vines. When this particular ex-SAS man had finished eight hours among the vines he was physically spent. I went off to soak my muscles in a hot bath and left him spread-eagled on the settee, where he remained the whole night unable to move his body in any direction without moaning. Oh, the years of fun my friends and I have had from that story! The SAS might be able to crush a grape, but as for picking them . . .

I would not have teased him so unmercifully had I known that a few days later he would be offering to buy my house. Luckily he has a sense of humour and fell in love with the French way of life almost immediately. I was amazed at his offer and so was his girlfriend, Annette, in London: it had not been in either of their plans for a future together. This had never seemed an appropriate way of life for Armani-suited Gary, who had always seemed more at home in the smart hotels of the world. However, the deed was done, and he had a new home and a new lifestyle almost overnight.

I was now in a position to buy my next house in France – but discovered that the owners had chosen to renege on the agreed price; sadly, many people in this life do not think that honesty pays. But luckily for them, my dead husband had woken up to smell the roses, well, the magnolia blossom actually. The ancient magnolia tree in the garden had called to me through that communication with Ian in the Exeter healing session. I really wanted this house and was feeling 'high' from my dose of angels, so I swallowed my pride and paid up. I find that quietly fuming only causes ulcers, so I just looked for the silver lining again.

There were silver linings bedecking this second house in France from day one. The first morning I went outside and found a bottle of wine and some fruit sitting on the doorstep. This was to be the first of many wonderfully generous gifts from the good people of the area: real old-fashioned, no-strings-attached friendship and hospitality. This was more like it – just like those early days in Ireland, when country people welcomed newcomers when they still knew nothing whatsoever about them. The tongue-in-cheek, self-deprecating sense of humour exhibited by the local farming community also reminded me of Ireland. When my nearest farming neighbour arrived on my doorstep holding his working hat respectfully in his hand I wanted to run and hide, certain that my French would not cope with whatever he was asking. In fact Guy and his lovely wife Nadine were just extending the hand of friendship by inviting me to join them for Sunday lunch. I went in trepidation, the sole Englishwoman amongst a family of fast-speaking locals. My first test was to recognise and admit to liking the delicious meal of roast hare. My second was to appreciate the superb wines accompanying each of the five courses. The final bonus was to survive a truly superb five-hour feast and remain upright all the way home across the field. I was to grow to feel very at home there.

I spent the first week with a sledgehammer knocking down the ugly fireplace that the previous owners had installed – just as well, really, because in the process I discovered that there was no accompanying flue to let the smoke out. While I was engaged on this filthy task I met my neighbour Julia, a feisty Spanish lady who was to become my firm friend, tutor and ally in dealing with local tradesmen and my new French life in general. She had heard the noise as I thundered my way through the chimney-breast. '*Est-ce que vous allez démolir toute la maison, madame, eh?*' (Are you going to knock down the whole house?)

She was really shocked at the mess that I was making, as she had thought that everything had been beautifully renovated and I would have nothing to do. But I was determined to make my mark, as people usually do in a new home; nostalgic for the old days of renovation in Ireland, I also thought that I could do it myself. I was enjoying all this demolition work until I reached the heavy timber that formed the mantelpiece, which was just too heavy for me to lift out of its resting place. I pulled, pushed and swore until I was exhausted, then did what I do when all else fails: I just sat down and cried with frustration amongst the dust and rubble. Where is a decent man when you need one? As chance would have it, my friends John and Chrissy arrived just as I was about to give the pile of rubble a good kicking. The three of us managed to haul the offending chunk of wood out to the garden before sharing an excellent burgundy that I just happened to have in the house. Good wine and good friends go a long way towards a happier life.

In among dealing with administrative paperwork and decorating I found time to look at many more spiritual theories from ancient civilisations and other dimensions or planes of the Universe, and had a great deal of enlightening fun on the journey. I am always happy to float off from day-to-day practicalities and read or learn from different experts about their diverse passions. Many cultures and civilisations across the centuries have used the techniques of energy medicine to heal and progress in life. It fascinates me to see how today's scientists are slowly coming back to re-evaluate and absorb the real value of the body's combined spiritual and physical power. I do think that the New Age revival of the sixties was a false start: those gentle flower power types who wanted to make love not war were perhaps on the right track, but they got diverted from their meditations by their quest for bigger and better mind travel. If only they had stayed with their own mental abilities, which could have given them just the mental 'trips' they sought, rather than allowing drugs into the equation, we might by now be living in a less damaging society.

People often ask me whether working with angels is a sort of cult or new religion. The answer is no; for me, it forms part of a psychological or spiritual journey towards self-discovery and is the way I personally interact with the greater Universe. In my mind I can hear those sceptics in the media who scorn as claptrap anything that smacks of self-discovery. Knowing that I myself came to this area as a sceptic, with both feet firmly on the ground, has helped many other people to understand a little more of what is available to them in times of need. It is not my intention to 'convert' anyone to anything, other than to learning just how special they themselves are. We are often more willing to accept our limitations than our strengths. I have met many people, especially those from my own background in the working-class homes of the sixties and seventies, who were taught not to get above themselves. Even the most loving of parents seemed to have felt it their job to teach children humility. There is nothing wrong with humility, of course – until we take it too far and deny our abilities to ourselves. To learn that we are our own best helper and can have a personal link to the angels or good spirits in another realm is a powerful piece of knowledge to possess in modern society. We may of course need some initial assistance in order to help ourselves, but that is fine. I was learning to accept help from many different people now that I realised that independence did not have to mean going it alone, no matter what.

My second house move in France took place in the middle of winter, so after I had finished knocking down chimneys I installed a very efficient log-burning stove and built a very French log pile. In the Périgord region of France one is not really respectable until there is a smartly stacked mound of logs outside, which needs to be covered by something called a *bâche*. I am fascinated by this French word for a groundsheet or a tarpaulin: is that where the British soldier stole the word 'basher' to denote his home? I suspect it was purloined during the First World War when soldiers used a ground-sheet or *bâche* for shelter in the trenches.

The house at Penot, meaning 'black hill', was to be the background to a very happy five years in my life. I had a group of friends who were French, English, Italian and Dutch, and together we formed a great *entente cordiale*. I loved the multicultural feeling of sharing and learning in such a mixed bunch. The place was curious for another little synchronicity: my old home in Ireland had also been on a black hill, named in old Irish Mullagdubh. The fact that Ian died on yet another hill – the hill of stone or Beinn na Lice on the Mull of Kintyre in Scotland – is yet another part of life's rich tapestry (or puzzle). I later came to live at the foot of the Sierra Blanca (white hills) in Spain – does this mean that life is going from black to white and upwards?

French life was not always smooth sailing, of course. I decided that I needed a swimming pool in the large garden, which was full of fruit trees and lots of grass – it would be more fun to swim up and down the lawn than to cut the grass. Learning to tackle French bureaucracy became a whole new area of frustration. It is interesting how people enter your life at just the right time for the next lesson or punishment, depending upon how you look at it.

The swimming-pool story, as told here, will be shorter than the saga it became. Suffice to say, I learned that I was not as strong and capable as I had grown to believe. I fell foul of a British installer, who started out as a seemingly respectable professional whom I chose because in those early days I did not trust my language skills enough to deal with a French company. But I regretted this decision when I could not get the final job finished to my satisfaction. The project that was to be a beautiful summer living area around the pool beside the orchard proved to be more difficult than I had ever envisaged.

I had asked for my pool to be finished for the anniversary of Ian's death on 2 June. It was in fact usable by this date, and I was happy until I spotted several problems that needed attention. So I refused to pay the last instalment, and as a result became victim to verbal bullying that I felt unable to deal with. I really did feel that being a lone female contributed to this situation and my confidence took a tremendous knock; I felt very vulnerable and more than a little silly to have been unable to resolve my own problems. I finally recouped only my legal expenses from the solicitor of the pool installer, who had since left the country. I suppose I could rationalise it by saying, if you don't make mistakes you're not working on hard enough problems, and that's a big mistake. I learned more lessons. Did he, I wonder?

I now possessed valued new friends, who had not known my husband and seemed to like me for myself; the circle of pals grew weekly and life was very full. During those next few years both of my children married and settled into their new lives with their respective partners, Sheena and Bob. One of many poignant moments happened for me during the wedding celebrations for Nicola and Bob. My friends Anne and Derek, whom I had met in France in the early days when we were all trying to improve our French with the same tutor, had flown to Belfast to be with us.

'You know,' said Derek, 'I'm so torn between my pleasure at being here and my disappointment that I never met Ian, because I know that if Ian were still alive we would probably never have met you and your family. I do so wish that I could have met him.' I knew what he meant, as Anne and Derek had indeed become part of our family circle just as their children had warmly welcomed me into their fun-filled and loving homes. I am eternally grateful for such good friends and the truly rich pleasures of life that we have shared; it is indeed another example of life's gifts to us after taking away the things we hold most dear. It is bizarre that Derek was to be the focus of Ian's attention in later years, as I shall explain in another chapter.

It was another very happy time when Niven and Sheena produced a daughter in the millennium year. I was so relieved and energised to see my son looking happier and more fulfilled than at any time since the death of his father. Thank heavens for new life. Bob and Nicola also started a new life in London and France, and I was proud and happy for them all.

I had started to feel content in my new French home, surrounded as I was by good friends and neighbours from both the French- and English-speaking communities who live in harmony in this pretty corner of rural France. For some years I had been practising my energy healing and angel relaxation techniques with friends and acquaintances on an ad hoc basis. Many people referred their pals to me if they had aching backs or odd pains that needed some gentle energy to ease whatever had caused them to feel unwell. It was a pleasure to help out in this way and feel that at last I was being useful in the world again. But at that time I was not asking for sufficient help from outside sources when doing such 'healings', and often found myself feeling drained because I gave too much of my own energy rather than seeking to channel universal energy from the other dimensions into the person seeking help. It was to take another course before I could over-rule my ego and accept help from angelic sources outside of myself – I needed to learn to ask for help for others, too. This knowledge was to grow within me during the increasingly deep meditations I found the time to do, and also when I essayed the larger world beyond my cosy hideaway. My sitting room became a happy, sunny oasis, with small pieces of crystal reflecting the light into the room like rainbows. Other, larger crystals spread their special energy into my living space, where I often burned essential oils and joss sticks to lighten and enhance the very positive energies that everyone enjoyed.

It was time for me to regain some confidence before venturing back to make a real contribution to life once more. What to do? A trip to London always seemed to go down well, and gave me an excellent excuse to have lunch with Nicola and Bob too. On my way to meet Nicola from her office I discovered quite by chance (another synchronicity?) a therapist in the New Age area of Neal's Yard, near Covent Garden. She was a regression therapist called Meg Pringle Adamson. I had been reading *Many Lives, Many Masters* by Dr Brian Weiss and thought I needed to investigate the concept of past lives for myself. Although I was not at all certain that I believed in reincarnation, I fancied some hypnotherapy anyway.

On the regression therapist's couch I was taken skilfully and gently into a deep trance-like state which was very relaxing and reassuring. I have a tape-recording of the process and know that I was not guided into anything other than my own mind by the therapist. I know many people will say I was taken into my own imagination rather than my subconscious, and I cannot disprove that; all I can state is that, had anyone asked me to write a story describing what I would expect to experience, none of the 'stories' that I experienced at the hands of the therapist would have borne any relation to what I had planned to write. The lives I saw were interesting and explained several features of my present life. In one life I seemed to be some kind of travelling soothsayer or medicine man – a man with a long grey beard. It appeared to be set in the Middle East, and I remember standing in front of a group of people in Arab robes who were watching me from a kind of amphitheatre.

When the therapist asked me what I felt from the crowd, I said, 'A lot of love and – oh yes, a mixture of cynicism.'

'Where do you live?' she asked.

I promptly burst out laughing as I lay there on the couch.

'What is it? Why are you laughing?' she asked.

'It's just that I seem to travel about and just stay with people.'

'So what's funny about that?'

I had suddenly been struck by the connection with my life now, in that I have always disliked staying in people's homes – even with really good friends. Ian and I had both always felt that we did not want to be a nuisance to others, and I still felt like this. I did not like to feel that I was taking advantage of people's good will in any way, and much preferred the anonymity of hotels wherever possible. Was this why?

Later, in that life as what appeared to be a man in the ancient Middle East, I was lying on a bed and could feel love and kindness on many faces around my bed who were looking at me with tears in their eyes. Suddenly I was rising upwards and feeling great, with an electrical fuzziness around my whole body.

'Oooh, lovely,' I said.

'Wait a minute. What are you doing?' said the therapist's voice from a long way off.

'I'm floating above my body and they're all crying down there – but it feels lovely. There's a big warm light waiting for me and arms stretching down – a voice saying, "Well done!" '

'No! Come back, come back. Don't go yet. Tell us more about what you've done in this life.'

I duly regrounded myself and talked some more about that

life as an old man where I appear to have been well loved but also scorned by some. The end result was always the same, though – the beautiful feeling of welcome and love and being told that I did well as I rose up. If that was death, then it will be all right when it eventually happens. If it was imagination, then it didn't do me any harm at all and I felt great afterwards.

Another 'life' that seemed to have connections with today was yet another dying experience. This time I appeared to be about fourteen years old and my parents were at the side of my bed in a poor, earth-floored home. I started to cough like a heavy smoker – it sounds a really sick cough, when I hear it on the tape. They were offering me scented herbs and oils to sniff. The therapist asked me what my father did for a living. I looked around the stone-walled room and saw crossbows, spears and shields propped against the wall; small children were also playing in the corner in the dirt.

'Why, my father's an armourer,' I said, sounding surprised. I have always had a fascination in this life with militaria and weapons, and my teenage experiences with archery and rifle shooting sprang to mind immediately. I had practised both when I was sixteen for my Duke of Edinburgh's Award Scheme. I had also loved visiting an old smithy with my dad to watch the carthorses being shod; the smell of the hot irons in the fire was almost a part of this regression, I thought. Nevertheless, there I was floating upwards again – whatever potions those kindly, loving parents were offering were not curing my life-threatening cough.

'*Ah, quel dommage,*' I sighed.

'What?'

'I said, "What a pity."'

'No, you didn't. You said "*dommage*".'

'Oh – I said it in French. I must have been in medieval

France at the time.' That could have explained, I thought, why I felt so much at home in the lovely region of south-west France with its medieval castles and rustic stonework. I suddenly remembered that sigh of relief I had felt as I reached Angoulême when making my first journey to France alone. I also mused that, whenever I need to rest or am under pressure (as I was immediately after Ian's death), I develop a chest and throat infection and the same cough that I had during my regression. Life's messages from another time, perhaps. So yet another life seemed to have some impact on me today.

As I was brought back to my life today I could clearly see my parents as they waited for my birth, and could feel their fear as I looked down. They were obviously frightened, waiting in their little bedroom in Peterborough. The skilled therapist was able to reassure me that it was safe to come back into the body that is now my own, and once more to feel the love that my parents had shared with me all their lives. As I left the therapist's room I couldn't wait to phone my sister and ask her about my birth. Pauline had been sent to the ever-helpful Elsie Yates next door while I entered the world, but she remembered it well. She was able to tell me that Mum and Dad were indeed very scared, because our mother had suffered a lot at my sister's birth and they had not planned for another baby, feeling as they did that she was getting too old for more children.

The next step from the regression therapist was to contact someone whose address she had given me for what I had thought to be a course in hypnotherapy training. It was in fact a very fashionable area of mind–body training called NLP, or neuro-linguistic programming, to give it its full title. This course to become an NLP practitioner was very useful to me – not because I wanted to practise NLP, but for all the things that I learned about myself. Ian McDermott, the highly professional course leader, explained that 'Neuro' refers to neurology – how mind and body are linked through the nervous system; 'Linguistic' is about language – how we influence each other and ourselves through language; and 'Programming' is about repeated sequences of thought and behaviour – how we act to achieve our goals, and the consequences of our actions. The focus is on individual choice and ability. Although I liked to irritate the course assistants by saying that NLP stood for 'Normal Living Programme' I enjoyed every part of this fascinating course, not least because it involved a lot of observation of my favourite non-verbal behaviours. I had studied both language acquisition and behaviour for my first degree, and had also applied it practically with my deaf clients and their families. The course reassured me that I did have useful skills to share with the world, and gave me the opportunity to meet a range of people across society that I had almost forgotten about, living in my quiet corner of France. Many of them were those thrusting young professionals who strive so hard to 'be something' in the world and whom I had not encountered for some time. It came as a surprise to me to realise how easy it was to help them relax and come to terms with their lives in a more satisfying manner after spending a little time on a course like this. It was extraordinary how many of these intelligent people felt the need to role-play in their professional lives: they felt they were inadequate for their jobs and that they needed to act out how they ought to behave as a certain person in a certain position. How sad that they could not be happy to be themselves because of preconceived ideas of what 'type' of person does certain jobs in society.

My biggest discovery came about during one of the 'settling down' exercises, during which Ian McDermott would use his voice to relax a group of a hundred and more students at a time. He truly is a master of hypnosis, or at least of his version of calming to induce a trance-like state of relaxation and self-induced mental imagery. He asked us to relax and imagine that we were walking towards a distant fairground, which could be from anywhere in our life or an imaginary one. I was there immediately, riding on a carousel, going round and round happily in my head. Suddenly my parents were standing watching me alongside my husband Ian – they were all smiling at me with that mixture of pride and love that we show towards our families (or should do). Then Ian McDermott was telling us that it was time to leave the fairground and walk away. Oh no, I didn't want to leave. I was basking in this feeling of love and warmth and I couldn't leave. But I did, reluctantly, and started to walk away. I wanted to take them all, physically, with me. As I walked away from this imaginary carousel that I suppose represented my previous life, an amazing thing happened. I had the real feeling that all three of my dead loved ones came and filled me with their love, as if to say, 'We are always there for you. Go on in strength now, knowing you have our strength with you, and do some bigger and better things in your life.' It was as simple as that. If that was all I learned on that course, with no talk of angels or spirits, it was worth every penny. Well, there was no 'official' talk about angels but I reckon Ian McDermott knows a few.

I went off on holiday that year to stay with another new friend to whom I had been introduced by way of yet another synchronicity in France. My friends Clive and Diana were an Anglo-Canadian couple who had been active in the media in both Britain and Vancouver before retiring to south-west France. It was in their home that I was to meet aspects of my past and future during one of the many lunch and dinner parties that were so much part of all of our lives there. I met part of my past in the form of Liz, the ex-drill corporal from my nursing days, who also reminded me of the Cambridge Military Hospital ghost stories. She and her husband had left their medical careers to retire early amongst the vineyards, and we were delighted to meet again so far from our roots. A few weeks later I was to meet Marion, a dynamic business-woman from Vancouver. She was a close friend of Clive and Diana's and we enjoyed each other's sense of humour immediately. Here was yet another woman who was able to live a fulfilled and happy life alone and enjoy life without complaining. She had brought up two handsome and intelligent sons who were a credit to single parenthood.

So it was to share a touring holiday with Marion in Canada that I set off. 'Wait till you hear the sound of the loons over the lakes,' she said, full of enthusiasm, as we drove through soft, rolling hills dotted with sagebrush and pine trees – real cattle country. We were on our way through the Cariboo country to the beautiful Rocky Mountains that divide British Columbia from Alberta. As I marvelled at the majestic mountains all around us, I saw brown bears and their cubs alongside the road. But before we actually reached the mountains, to Marion's surprise she found herself in a very small boat drinking cosmopolitan cocktails and eating salmon and crisps while we rowed ourselves around the loon lake. I can see her face now as she kept repeating, 'I can't believe I'm doing this – dammit!' I had insisted on going fishing, something she had not done since she was a child, and I think that secretly she felt this was not quite fitting behaviour for two middle-aged ladies. We compromised by taking the boat out without the rods – hence the cocktails, so that we felt a little more grown up. Our girlish shrieks of delight were definitely heard by the loons (better known in Britain as grebes) when we witnessed a fish jump of its own free will into the boat of a family who were rowing past us in the middle of the lake. What fun, and she was right about the sound of the loon – this ungainly bird makes the most enigmatic cry as it swoops over the water before doing a very inelegant belly-flop landing.

As we toured this awesome country I so enjoyed anticipating each new town as it leapt from my ever-ready map to reality. The town names were so foreign and yet so familiar to me from the old black-and-white films – Kamloops, Kelowna and Revelstoke on the Canadian Pacific railway line. I remember becoming quite emotional and going back to my girlhood again, thinking how much my dad would have enjoyed Revelstoke with its railway museum. I could almost smell the soot of the old steam engines on display, much larger than those that I had so admired all those years ago in Peterborough. The enormous present-day engines still haul their carriages right through the town with neither fence nor barrier.

When we reached the Rockies we visited another magical place – Banff. I had already read the tourist information and looked forward to a trip on the ski lifts high into the pure, crisp summer air, but I was not prepared for the sight of crystal-clear Lake Louise far below us or the feeling of great energy that came to me up there. How disappointed we were not to be able to stay at the famous Château Hotel, or 'Shatoo' as my Canadian friends insist on calling it; I really wanted to stay longer. I have since learned that Banff is supposedly the etheric retreat of the Archangel Michael. Michael, the warrior angel and usually depicted with sword and shield, is a favourite of mine – not just because I have always had a weakness for warriors of one sort or another, either. Known as the Angel of the North, he guards you against danger from that direction and protects your throat chakra with his blue ray of healing. Lake Louise has a beautiful blue reflection from somewhere out of this world – is it Michael's blue ray? Who can say, but it adds to the glorious memories for me.

In late 2001 another Michael, not the Archangel (I think!), in France, suggested that it was perhaps time for me to try another angel course. His words were something like, 'Not heard much about the angels recently, darling – gone off them, have we?' Michael and his partner Raymond had become very good friends to me over the preceding years and had contributed much fun and laughter, not to mention intelligent guidance, to my new life. When Michael speaks, people listen. I looked up Diana Cooper on the Internet, and there she was with another selection of weekend angel teaching courses just ready and waiting for me. So it was that a winter weekend in 2001 found me taking the chilly route north once more. I never seem to get it right, going north in winter and south in summer. My ambition had always been to go south with the swallows in the autumn, and this was something I would eventually achieve.

12

Crystals and Energy from Ancient Roots

A crisp winter weekend in Somerset was the start of yet another upturn for my personal journey, as a motley crew came together to learn how to teach people about angels and ascension. This proved another surprise to me, as I had not really thought about the course content or even its title: I just felt that I needed another dose of angels. I had continued to use some of the healing techniques learned on that first angel course, several years before, to great effect; my speciality seemed to be taking the pain from friends' tennis elbows. My angel cards were an essential part of my travelling kit and had also become *de rigueur* for friends who came to dinner. It used to be after-dinner mints, and now it was, 'Anyone fancy an angel card?' I have several sets of such cards designed by different people, and it is interesting to see how, if you repeat the question several times even with different packs, the angels give you the same answers. Even the toughest cynics tended to ask for a card – 'just for fun', they would say. As with many of the training and educational courses we under-take in life, the people we meet there often contribute as much to our learning and enjoyment as the tutor. So it was to be with this first of many action-packed weekends. Diana Cooper brought her marvellous energy of angels into a diverse group of interesting, spirited and intelligent students. To manage such a group takes some skill and all the help that other-worldly energies, be they angels or spirits, can bring to each day's class. Each strong and beautiful personality in the room seemed to have a point to make, whether the point was relevant to the group learning or not. I love such character-filled groups for the fun they provide and the challenge they present. Diana managed them all in her inherently cool and competent way, and it was a pleasure to watch.

I was so happy to be back with a group with whom I could discuss the parallel worlds of angels and healing spirit energy without receiving 'There she goes again' looks. I knew that being part of a coherent Universe of spiritual energies combined with love, clear emotion and physical truth was a good place to be. After all, I had Diana to thank for bringing me, or at least a large part of my soul, back to this world six years earlier. Without the knowledge of the supportive love available to my inner being from the 'other realms' I would probably have taken much longer to find my way to the happier new life in France. I could so easily have remained a needy, grieving person seeking love and comfort from anyone or anywhere if Diana had not shown me that we could seek personal support from an angelic presence all by ourselves. Since that time I had continued to research worldwide spiritual beliefs and personal stories until I felt happy with the inner truth that worked for me. I arrived in Somerset feeling relatively content and whole, but still found a lot to stimulate my inner learning and development yet again.

The GALA mnemonic for my philosophy of life that I mentioned in the Introduction (gratitude, acknowledgement, love and laughter, and acceptance) reminds me that, although personal pain from loss or other life trauma and desperation often plays a part in our search for help and change from new support systems, gratitude plays an even bigger part as we develop. I have found that the more often I acknowledge help and say thank you, the more good things occur in my life. When things have gone wrong for me they have often done so at times when I have been complaining or fighting against something that didn't suit me at the time. It is a bit like disappearing down a negative plug-hole if we complain about everything and forget to be grateful for the truly good things that happen, no matter how small or insignificant. We have to remind ourselves to admire that baby's smile or those birds singing in the treetops. We need to look for things to be grateful for. As we dash along on a wet day with our heads down, moaning about the weather, we are more likely to get splashed by a passing car or bump into a lamppost. Yet if we try to acknowledge that the gardens need the water and there are some quite interesting patterns in the puddles, we are more likely to be ready for that chance encounter with a friend or to see something great in a shop window that pleases us.

On this and other angel teaching weekends in Somerset I rediscovered the power and peace of meditation in a group. I often have problems trying to meditate deeply when alone, and the extra power gained by pooling all that mental energy in a group is fantastic. Diana started the weekend by re-minding us that one does not need to be psychic to see or feel angels, though one does need to be intuitive, grounded and have faith and integrity – schizoid psychics need not apply! Intuition is not necessarily imagination, but rather having faith in your own inner knowledge and perceptions. It can be likened to remembering a contract you made before entering this life: did we all elect to do a job here on earth? We need to think about just how society has encouraged us to block out our real awareness of what is around us. Group norms really do shape our consciousness. How can we believe that our children's 'imaginary' friends are real to them, and perhaps to another dimension too, when our whole socialisation process has taught us to distrust such a concept? The same applies to ghosts and the spirit world, never mind angels. Once such topics are raised in discussion with friends and even comparative strangers an extraordinary number of people admit to having had spiritual experiences that they cannot explain. These admissions are often preceded by disclaimers such as 'I know it sounds nutty or stupid but . . .', which means the people concerned have regulated or hidden the experience to suit their own comfort zone. Since the Middle Ages the tenets of acceptable social behaviour have herded people away from their own intuition or sixth sense: it was easier to burn witches and heretics, for independent free spirits were not welcome in the developing world of control.

I can go a step further here to introduce the idea that it is not just our inner selves that are self-regulating, but that we live on a self-regulating planet. We are not isolated units suspended on this earth for self-gratification. At long last scientists are discovering that the earth does behave like a self-regulating system in which life and its material environment are massively interconnected; Gaia theory is now an acceptable area of scientific research, according to James Lovelock. The fact that many scientists still refer to this research as earth system science or biogeochemistry is irrelevant to me. What they are using in Gaia, even indirectly, is the ancient name of the earth goddess. The holistic approach is beginning to unite scientists in the common cause of a rational environmentalism; in other words, we affect our planet and our planet affects us. Meditation and the raising of group energies to a more positive level have a serious effect on the earth energy. Before many group meditations people often use Lady Gaia as a grounding centre to keep the meditation firmly earthbound: it is a stabilising concept, I feel, to suggest that we put our roots down into the centre of the earth to anchor and wrap around a beautiful crystal belonging to Lady Gaia. Crystals from the earth are becoming much more valued as contributors to life these days. When we are well centred and grounded like this, acknowledging the central beauty of the earth and the healing crystals it contains, we can float off in our mind's eye to wherever we need to go to bring peace and contentment to our very souls. Sounds weird to you? That's fine – but have you tried it?

After my first course on angels and ascension I travelled to see my daughter and astonished her by having 'seen' things she was doing in my absence. This next course was to be even more powerful and to show me new ways of becoming 'high' on my own brainpower – and not a drop of wine in sight. Having fun and sharing the joy of it all is really uplifting. Remember, angels fly because they take themselves lightly; we can go higher when we clear out many of the old mental blockages that hold us back until we go deeper into our true selves. I was feeling very balanced and centred when I arrived, but knew that I would surely learn more about myself as the days progressed. But this is not what some people want – it can be easier to hide behind whatever façade we build for ourselves. Rather like clearing memorabilia from a fusty old cupboard it can be difficult, even painful, to let go, but we need the room in order to move on. Asking ourselves how much rubbish is stored in our own minds can be painful, but it is often necessary to clear it out in one way or another before we can move forward in a constructive way.

There were indeed some very special participants in the group, and I made some great friends, many of whom have continued to communicate with me over the years since. One person I shall never forget was a wonderful young woman who at the time was fighting a recurrence of cancer. This delightful soul was divorced with two young children and yet remained cheerful and hopeful throughout. One of our exercises involved making healing balls of energy in our hands, using our own and universal 'angel' energy. The exercise involved moving around the room with our arms full of energy and then zapping this energy into the aura or energy field of another person. There were twenty-four people and simple maths would suggest that twelve people should give energy to the other twelve in the room. When the exercise appeared to be finished Diana asked if everyone had given and received a zap of energy. Only one person had not been given anything, and, bizarrely, that was our colleague with the cancer. However, at this time only a few of the other students knew that she was suffering at all. Diana then asked everyone to make a new energy ball by calling on the healing angels and any other energy that we felt suitable. It was an emotional time for me and those others who knew about our new friend as we all queued up in front of this shining personality to give her our personally made doses of angel healing; each person spontaneously hugged her as they offered their gift. Was it a synchronicity of the Universe that she had escaped one dose of healing in order to receive twenty-three powerful doses of healing energy from the angels of the Universe with our additional love? Her beaming, dreamy smile at the end was a great reward for even the most cynical in the group.

Each participant had something new and good to contribute to the group. Two students had brought along their own healing treasures to help us all broaden our horizons, and I encountered my first crystal-healing bowl alongside the most interesting piece of clear quartz I had seen. Soon I understood much more about the powerful energy given out by crystals or gems and minerals that had been growing for millions of years in the centre of the earth. As a child I had been fascinated by stones and rock formations in the ground; as a schoolgirl I had really enjoyed geography lessons that focused on geology; and as a young mum I had taken my own children on fossil expeditions to the seashore. Now, as a middle-aged woman, I was learning for the first time how such beautiful bounty from the earth could be used to help the human body and spirit. I discovered that using crystals could help to loosen energy blocks in the body: the individual vibrations of gemstones can be used to balance chakras and also to diagnose imbalance. What they cannot usually do is actually replace medical help, but used alongside medicine in a holistic approach they can provide wonderful support to patients. Crystals can activate the healing process of the physical body with the help of vibrations and harmony, along the same principles as acupuncture and acupressure where the body's energy lines or meridians are aligned. On my trip to Canada a year earlier I had already accidentally discovered that I was sensitive to crystal energy. In a gemstone shop in Vancouver, looking for some simple amethyst jewellery for my daughter and daughter-in-law, I suddenly felt overcome with a tremendous headache. I apologised to the shop assistant for wanting to pay quickly and leave as I had a sore head.

'Oh, sure, ma'am,' she responded. 'That's pretty common in here as a result of all those huge crystals around the walls. Some folks are particularly sensitive to their energy!'

I looked up from the counter to admire the wonderful array of enormous crystals from British Columbia and around the world that, in my haste to buy presents, I had ignored, and immediately bought a very palm-fittingly satisfying piece of amethyst to put in my home. I was to discover that we are always attracted to the crystal that we need at that moment – if it attracts you, there is a good chance that you need it to balance some aspect of your psyche. A crystal that feels good to touch and warms in your hand is going to be good for you. Later I discovered that [amethyst is considered to be good for headaches and migraines as well as nervous aches and tension] I had automatically reached for what I needed that day – just as, all those years earlier in Ireland, Vivienne, the skilled kinesiologist, had known that I needed a lump of rose quartz on my solar plexus. This lovely pink mineral is (especially useful for absorbing fears and healing psychic wounds of the heart, stimulating our ability to accept and love others as well as ourselves. It is also reported to help us regain tenderness and open our feelings for creative thinking. Behind me on my mantelpiece now, as I work, I have three large chunks of crystal overlooking me. One is an enormous piece of rose quartz (which I hope helps my creativity and keeps my heart in balance), a large amethyst (giving me concentration, keeping headaches at bay and the crown chakra open for inspiration from above), and a transparent, clear quartz crystal (which supposedly clarifies and harmonises the aura, taking away any disturbing energies in my living space). This rock crystal also works with the third eye, the chakra in the middle of the forehead, and for eye complaints, so that should help my spelling. If you look around your own home and into your jewellery box you may be surprised at just what you have felt a subconscious need for at different times; it can be fun as well as therapeutic to consider what you have acquired during your life, when, and why.

It is no coincidence, I feel, that I never possessed a diamond until my fifty-fifth birthday. A friend and I were looking at gems in a shop in Hawaii when I mentioned that I had never owned a diamond. She looked at me in a pitying way and said, 'Never mind – someone will buy you one, one day!' As if one always has to wait for someone else to give you happiness, I thought. I immediately found a tiny diamond simply set in titanium and bought it for myself. Life is what you make it today, and you can make it for yourself and others without waiting to be 'given to'. The fact that diamonds are used by healers seemed to be appropriate. My precious engagement ring, bought thirty-five years ago, was a sapphire. I have already passed it on to my daughter to allow the power of the sapphire to help in her life path. I like the fact that sapphire is often referred to as the philosopher's stone; also that J. K. Rowling chose to mention it in her Harry Potter books and that there is a phoenix feather involved. If we look hard enough, there is always something that makes a connection with our past and future. We just have to learn to look for the links. My imagination, you say? If it is only that, it gives me a great deal of fun and pleasure and that is fine by me. But are you sure?

On that same holiday in Hawaii I was lucky enough to have a Watsu massage from Lynne Starke, a very gifted and skilled therapist of this particular form of massage/manipulation. A kind of Shiatsu massage done underwater, the technique can be used to treat a variety of physical ailments, including arthritis, back pain, joint pain and chronic fatigue, as well as some neurological disorders. According to the American Physical Therapy Association, Watsu can help decrease pain, muscle tension, stress levels and blood pressure. Practitioners also report that Watsu can help patients sleep better and give them a sense of wellbeing.

Watsu is said to touch you at all levels. I had been surprised in my first session, a year previously, to feel as though I had regressed to the womb. This is not surprising once you discover how the body is moved about in the water during a Watsu session. Lynne asked me to imagine I was a rag doll and just let go. I felt as though I was not only in a meditative state but also floating out of the womb and into the air, almost like flying through a star gate into the Universe beyond our world. In fact I saw an image like the star constellation of the Pleiades coming towards me, and I felt wonderfully light and happy. On this second session, a year later, I was looking forward to something equally beautiful, but when we try to repeat great experiences they do not always live up to our expectations. I had this in mind, of course, when I should have been switching off my cognitive mind and slipping into a meditative state as Lynne applied her skilful moves to my limbs in the water.

Suddenly I felt my arm shoot up in the air straight out of the water – I had been drifting off, and this movement almost brought me out of the trance-like state that I was actually enjoying in spite of my preconceptions. My middle finger was zapped by an intense electrical impulse. Lynne tells me that I stayed like that for several minutes as a beatific smile spread across my face and I glowed my way around the warm pool water. When she eventually woke me up where she had gently rested my floppy body at the side of the pool she too was grinning happily at me and saying how wonderful it had been for her to watch. That finger has become an interesting signal to me when there is spirit activity around, almost as though it gets plugged into another source of energy in another dimension. It does not worry me and is a source of fascination as I begin to wonder just what other signals we can use to benefit our own energy system. Once we start to use all of our senses at optimal level, who knows where it leads us? It is part of us and of our own growing knowledge of the Universe and ourselves.

It can be exciting getting in touch with tactile senses and

sounds to see how such things resonate with our very heart and soul.

Back at the angel teaching weekend in Somerset I saw and heard used for the first time the beautiful healing bowl made from ground-down crystal; it was baked hard into a bowl shape, which can be made to resonate a rich tone by striking it with a crystal pestle. This tone can actually raise the inter-acting vibrations of someone's energy field to such a rate that they can enter a trance-like state. I was later to discover a link with some serious diagnostic work being carried out in Bergerac in south-west France by a psychic shop owner with a complete set of such marvellous bowls, each resonating at a different frequency depending upon their size.

One of the more life-changing scenes that I witnessed on that weekend happened one morning as I sauntered along to pick up my yoga mat to start the morning exercise. As I reached the corridor where the mats were stacked, my attention was drawn into the next room by something bright. The room was actually part of an old chapel converted into a sunny seminar room in this very special centre. As I looked I saw Jenny, our feng shui expert and ghost buster, leaning over Kevin, who was sitting on a chair with his back to me. This alone would not have stopped me in my tracks. It was what I perceived to be an amazing golden light, together with a third figure made of light, behind Jenny, blending itself all over the two figures, that held me spellbound. It was as if the two (or was it three?) figures were in a golden frame. Had I not seen it myself, I would not have believed it. As I watched, Jenny continued to work down the energy centres (chakras) of Kevin's body in a soothing and structured way, not touching him but interacting with his aura (energy field) by placing her flat hand over each chakra point of his body, clearing and cleaning as she went. I was familiar with this technique, having used it myself to help people feel the soothing power of their own body energy interacting with the universal energy from their environment and beyond. We can soothe another person's mental state by using our hands to interact with their body's energy field in a gentle manner. If we choose to call in an angel energy to help we can do so, and the results can be very powerful. To date I had felt but not seen, so to speak. I now know that we can be allowed to see this wonderful interaction of two people's energy by using my aura camera with a computerised output, but that was unknown to me in 2002. One of the pioneers of aura photography, Guy Coggins, has developed a system linking Kirlian photography and sensory hand plates to a computer. The resulting images displayed on screen show the energy interaction between individuals' auras. Inexplicable phenomena often appear as other energies enter the aura.

On this sunny winter morning I witnessed the most amazing sight of visual energy, and was unable to decide whether Jenny had grown a wing or if there was a third person in the room. As she worked, Kevin's energy field visibly changed size, pulsating all around his body; it was clear and bright to my naked eye. When Jenny called upon a healing angel to come in to help I actually saw an enormous beam of light arrive from outside the building and form a ball of golden light at Kevin's throat area, and immediately the throat chakra became enormous as I heard Jenny whisper, 'Thank you.' They continued with this healing for several minutes and I could not pull myself away from the extraordinary sight. As they finished, I saw the aura settle down to a uniform glow all around Kevin as he smilingly turned with emotion to thank Jenny. As he stood, they hugged each other and turned simultaneously to discover this tear-stained eavesdropper transfixed in the doorway. All three of us then hugged each other, with tears pouring down our cheeks at the sheer beauty of an experience in which we had all been participants. 'Wow!' I said. 'I've never seen such a tremendous aura before.'

'Don't tell everyone,' joked Kevin, 'or I'll get no peace tonight.' 'Kevin's massive aura' remained a nudge-nudge joke for some time!

In spite of his ability to joke about it, he was floating about mentally for the rest of the day. At one stage I was sitting beside him before a group meditation and he grabbed my arm to ask if I could ground him as he was not sure he could take much more of this ecstasy. On that evening we did a small group meditation using an Om, a chant used to induce a meditative trance that allows the inner self to experience great peace; and to my amazement his whole body had indeed moved upwards visibly, beyond his six-foot height, by the end of the session. It was a good day for Kevin and he felt renewed for the rest of the weekend. I was so moved by the whole experience that I drew a sketch of what I had seen, as I did not want to forget the beautiful vision that I had been allowed to witness.

A final memory of that weekend was an exercise that I did with two other students, Jeanie and our friend recovering from cancer. We all sat down in a circle and held each other's hands, overlapping in a little pile in the centre. Leaning forwards with our eyes closed, we then posed silent personal questions on guidance to our guardian angels. During the course of this mini-meditation I felt that I was being asked if I would give my life to let the shining spirit of my colleague live. It was not a hard question to reply to: she was a young woman who had everything to live for, with a young family who needed her and a very important project for small children with which she was involved. Yes, of course I felt that she had more to give to the earth than I at that moment. I answered what I perceived to be my angel's question and sat back, leaving my hands in the centre. Jeanie also sat back, and we beamed at each other as we watched our sick friend basking in what appeared to be a golden glow of happiness as she continued beaming to herself for another five minutes. When she eventually pulled out of this little trance she looked at me and said, 'Oh, Susan, I hope you don't mind – but I think I've just taken some of your energy. You seemed to have loads of love and light when I was in the middle of it, and I couldn't stop just basking in the warmth and bright light of it all.' I, of course, replied that she was very welcome to share whatever I had. Even more surprisingly, both Jeanie and I then revealed that whoever or whatever we had been communicating with had asked us the same question. We had both said yes for the same reasons, and felt good about it. What an intense and yet pleasurable experience we had shared. I can still feel the warmth that it brought to us all – better than happy pills any day.

Significant things always happen to me on angel courses, and yet another synchronicity occurred at one of these teaching weekends. Diana asked us to write an essay, and as I read mine again recently I remembered another wonderful experience in a medieval abbey in the Limousin area of France. I actually wrote the essay in February 2002 and noted the significance of the date, because at 8.02 p.m. that day a unique complete date occurred in the twenty-four-hour clock: 2002 2002 2002. The time, day, month and year synchronised beautifully, never to be repeated in time or space. What has this to do with angels? I am uncertain, but it seemed worth noting at the time.

When I began my journey home to France from the Somerset course I was extremely elated, feeling the angels' energy in my car as they jostled for space on the back seat. In fact I actually spoke to them as though they were excited children going on holiday. There was a distinct air of happiness and energy in the car. Just as I was approaching Limoges good old Michael rang to say that he had been feeling quite ill since I had spoken with him in London. I then happened to say that perhaps his guardian angel had joined mine for the trip to France. We jokingly suggested that I should send his angel back to him before I went any further. I also said that my car seemed to be full of a variety of angels – whom we both agreed were very wise to be coming south with me at this time of year. He casually suggested that I would be better to avoid the main route through Limoges, where I normally crossed to another motorway. His parting words were, 'Take the road further south, and don't forget to send back my angel!'

I took his advice, but mistook the turning and found myself on an unknown route. As I meandered through the narrow lanes I thought of turning back, but a voice urged me forward on to what looked like the road to nowhere. I eventually came into a beautiful medieval village, Solognac, with a huge abbey in the centre. By this time the energy in the car was tremendous, with what seemed to be a bunch of very excited angels all wanting to go inside the abbey. I felt drawn to this lovely old building and got out to investigate. The main door was closed to visitors so I wandered round looking for another, and eventually found one marked as St Michael's door. As soon as I entered I heard a heavenly choir in full flow, although I could see no one. I felt the angels swooping in ecstasy around the roof as I sat quietly in one of the ancient choir stalls to absorb the atmosphere.

The singing actually came from a Benedictine friary at-tached to the abbey, according to the notices I read outside, and it was their lunchtime prayers and hymns that I could hear. Knowing I had a six-hour drive ahead I reluctantly left this peaceful haven, only a few miles from traffic-choked Limoges, and silently thanked my pal Michael whose saint's door I had used to enter this great resting place. It was understandably difficult to get the angels back in the car, and yet I felt the energy level rise when I closed the car door. As I drove slowly out of the village I was still not sure if it was the right direction, but I knew that I was heading roughly south-west and so it could not be too far out of my way.

I began thinking about a conversation I had had with Diana, on the last evening of the course, about the Camino de Saint Jacques de Compostela in Spain; she had talked of her wish to walk this old pilgrims' route one day. I had been a little dismissive in stating that it was hard walking over mountaintops and it might be easier to do only parts of it, and even those in instalments; preferably staying in decent hotels rather than pilgrim hostels, I had thought to myself. I was obviously feeling in need of a little luxury at the time because I normally love hiking in the mountains, and I actually lived not far away from some of the French trails of this famous route. In the Middle Ages pilgrims came from all over Europe to visit the shrine of St Jacques (or St James as he is known to English speakers) in Santiago de Compostela in northern Spain. To this day people can be seen in the towns of that region wearing his emblem of a scallop shell (Coquilles St Jacques, perhaps more familiar from restaurant menus) as they retrace the route. Shirley Maclean's book about her journey along the Camino makes fascinating reading, and I have met many people who have related amazing tales of spiritual experiences while hiking this path. My mind was casually wondering if I could find some books on the local portion of the route when I thought I had better turn south in the next little village I reached.

The view round the next corner was much more than a coincidence: there it was, the first bridge of the old route in the Limousin area, several hundred kilometres north of my house. I had no idea it was there. I parked up and spent some time just standing there, feeling the pilgrims' spirit as they must have tramped across all those years ago. In the middle of this bridge, with a lovely midday light shining through, was an ancient cross erected to the memory of St Jacques. I am sure my angels arranged for me to have just enough spare camera space to take the final three photos of my journey.

How special it felt to be there totally alone in the February sunshine, and I know the accompanying angels felt so too. I thanked them before getting back into the car to follow roads over the hilltops of the Limousin area that I had never travelled before. It was so pretty, and such a privilege to discover this way home rather than take the often fraught autoroutes for the whole journey south. Do I think it was an angel route? Of course – why not? Michael certainly rang at the right time that day, and his angel must have returned home because he had fully recovered from his illness by that evening. My own angels continued to keep me company on the long drive home, which seemed to pass more quickly and joyfully than usual.

I can reflect now on something that I did not register at the time. Just after this course finished I learned that June, a friend I had met in France, had lost her husband. They had moved to southern Spain a few years earlier, and her husband had died on the local golf course as they finished a game. She told me that he had had a wonderful smile of peace on his face as he lay on the green in front of her, and she knew that he had gone somewhere beautiful. It was her own peace that she was now seeking, and we arranged for me to drive down to offer whatever comfort I could. It would take me two days because it was even further than from the Channel coast to my French home and I had not ventured on such a long solitary journey before, but it seemed like a good idea.

As I drove south towards Madrid I decided to stop over in Burgos, a gorgeous medieval city in northern Spain which, though it did not occur to me at the time, would have been on the pilgrims' route. As I continued on this journey I had the distinct feeling that Ian was sitting in the seat beside me. I had been feeling more emotional than I expected as the landscape changed from the misty, mirage-like plains before Madrid to the olive groves and red ochre-coloured soil further south. Perhaps it was because I had not been in this area since Ian and I visited it together twenty years before. Whatever it was, I received a serious addition to my synchronicity list when the all-Spanish radio station suddenly started to play 'The Mull of Kintyre' sung in English, just as I was asking the energy in my passenger seat if it could possibly be Ian. I took a deep breath, said, 'Thank you' and continued more confidently on my way towards the warm smell of pine trees and wild herbs. As I descended from the foothills of the Sierra Nevada I still had that tell-tale pressure in my ears that tells me Ian is around. I had a passenger for at least three hours, and he didn't need loo stops either.

Once I saw the sparkling blue Mediterranean and the breakers on the shoreline I could almost feel another new life approaching; more signs were appearing in my life. When I reached June's home we talked about these signs that I had seen or felt in the years since Ian's death and she said, 'I wish I could have evidence that Barry is happy where he is now.' I started talking about the significance of feathers, and how, when we feel low, asking for, and finding, a white feather can be a sign that angels are there to help us. She gasped as she looked across at her husband's favourite chair to see, nestling on the shiny brown leather, a pure little white feather. Now June is a far better housewife than I and there was no way she would have left something like that during her cleaning. Nor does she have a budgie or feather-filled pillows in her house. Where did it come from? On another day that winter a friend of hers rang from Devon to suggest that she should look out into the garden to see the last pink rosebud. She realised that her friend could not possibly have known that it was indeed there in her Spanish garden. The friend's husband is a psychic intuitive, and when June asked how they knew about it the reply was simply, 'Barry told me he sent it to you.'

If we stop to think about what happens to us on a daily basis it is possible to see that the other dimension is giving us messages about all manner of things. We need to become more aware of our own synchronisation with the energy of the world and how it interacts with our own aura. I thought about those old wives' tales that I heard my mother utter in an almost automatic way. If she shivered she would say, 'Ooh, someone's walking over my grave.' When the palm of her hand itched she would rub it and say, 'I must be coming into money', and if she had an ear that was tickling she would scratch it and say, 'Someone must be talking about me.' Where did these sayings originate? Perhaps earlier generations were better able to recognise and take comfort from such signs and messages. When there was less techno-logical disturbance to the energy patterns of the world the human aura would have been more susceptible, more in touch with outside stimuli from the rhythms of the Universe, and the other dimensions could send in their messages to help us along life's path.

Almost nine years since Ian's death I was sitting in a
restaurant on the Costa del Sol with the recently widowed
June when we met a couple who were sitting discussing a pile
of olive pits (or stones, depending on how you were raised)
after their evening meal. That's really all one has to do on a
warm, sleepy night on the Mediterranean coast. Our table
had been squeezed into one of those small restaurant windows that spill you on to the street and we were almost too
comfortably close to our fellow diners. June and I had been
discussing angels – doesn't everyone? – when in my usual
manner I decided to join the American couple's conversation
about their olive consumption. So over angels and olive
stones on the Costa del Sol we got to chatting with this
couple from Montana in the USA. I heard June asking the
woman, 'So do you believe in angels, then?' I was rather
taken aback that she should be asking a complete stranger a
question that still raised eyebrows in many environments,
and cautiously looked over my shoulder to see if men in
white coats were being called to take us away. Having
established that there were none about (men in white coats,
not angels), and that the woman was in fact now paying June
a lot of attention, I proceeded to ask the husband the same
question in a somewhat laid-back and tentative manner: 'I
suppose you think this is rubbish?'

What a wonderful surprise when Richard, as he introduced himself, smiled warmly and said, 'Listen, young lady,'
(I loved him for that), 'in my line of business you had to
believe or you didn't do your job right.'

'What line of business would that be?' I asked, sitting
slightly back in my chair as I wondered what bizarre occupation he might have followed.

'Why, neuro-surgery,' he stated.

I heaved a mixed sigh of relief and mounting excitement:

'Would you like to share what exactly you mean with me, please?'

Richard went on to explain that, as a young surgeon, one of the first things he learned from a senior colleague was that if he heard patients tell him that they knew they would die on his operating table they would almost certainly do so. He was told that he must not put it down to poor surgical technique or anything else of this world, but to an individual's premonition of death: when people really knew they were going to die, the experienced surgeon confirmed to him, they usually did. Richard told me of a brother and sister who were very close to each other. One weekend they both had a similar dream in which the brother died in a horrific water-skiing accident on the local lake on what appeared to them both to be the following Friday. Sure enough, the young man ended up hitting his head while out on the lake that day and was taken unconscious to Richard's hospital. After what seemed a simple operation he did not recover as expected, and died the next day. His heartbroken sister later recounted the dream to Richard and was certain that it was a premonition that became fact. Richard knew many stories like that, and had no doubt that there was another dimension to this world that we catch glimpses of from time to time. When I asked if he had presented professional papers to colleagues on the topic he said that he had, and that the audiences were always divided between those who believed and those who preferred to remain sceptical for their own comfort. I have personally found that those who ridicule any subject outside their own knowledge or experience are those most frightened of change and growth. It is not surprising that for a very long time many people thought the world was flat. The wise are those who say that, although they have never experienced certain things, they are willing to accept that there are always possibilities.

There were two outcomes to this particular chance meeting in Spain. First, I started to think about writing this story; and secondly, at around the same time I realised that perhaps I could follow the swallows to the Mediterranean one winter soon.

13
Touched by a Spirit

I had started to mull over the idea of writing about the many weird and wonderful things that had happened in my life since Ian's death when I found myself with the task of organising a Diana Cooper angel teaching course in France. The first thing was to drive around the beautiful Périgord region looking for suitable hotels. I had tentatively booked one just outside the town of Bergerac when the hoteliers suddenly announced a huge price increase. I drove away in fury, not quite sure where I was going, then suddenly came across a rather grand sign for an hotel I did not even know existed. Curiosity drew me onwards along narrow country lanes that I had never driven before until there in front of me stood a fine château set in a gracious landscape with its own lake and stable block. I thought it was perfect, but doubted that the budget would stretch to such an imposing venue. However, I have never been shy about asking for anything on someone else's behalf (another of my dad's expressions was 'If you don't ask, you don't get'). The owners of Le Grand Vignoble were only too pleased to accept our booking at rates we could afford and even volunteered to open a few days early, after their winter break, to accommodate us. They were charming and welcoming, and not even fazed by the special dietary requirements requested by many of the students. This, in rural France, even in a very smart hotel, is unusual. In the south-west the three-course menu is quite often duck, duck and duck – not to mention foie gras! Not here, however: the chef stood on his head to accommodate everyone's needs with the most delicious and inventive menus possible. This experience illustrated to me, yet again, that when one door closes in disappointment a much better door is often just waiting to open.

We were a few days into the course and it was 1 April – no, this is not an April fool joke that I am about to tell, even if it sounds like one. Just before lunchtime we were all sitting in a circle and doing something that needed us to pay attention to the files on our laps. I had started to feel very odd – the tingling all over my scalp, radiating down my arms and legs and into my toes, was taking my concentration away from whatever Diana was telling the group. I suddenly thought that I had had this feeling before: when Ian had visited me at four in the morning just after he had died, and also during regression therapy when I had felt as though I were floating heavenwards. Wondering whether I was about to drop dead, I called across the room to interrupt Diana.

'Excuse me – is anyone in the room clairvoyant?' I asked.

'Oh, my God!' I heard someone say.

'Wow!' said Diana, as she raised her head to look at me across the circle.

'What is it?' I could feel myself starting to grin foolishly and happily as my tingles continued to warm my whole body beautifully.

'Well, I've never seen an angel or anything quite like that before,' Diana said in her usual matter-of-fact way. I always love the way Diana can talk about an angelic presence as if it were a loaf of bread. She went on to explain what she could see, confirmed by heads nodding in agreement from her side of the room. 'It's a massive golden presence all over and above you, reaching to the ceiling.'

'And there's someone – a figure – standing beside it,' said a new voice – an Irish voice from Belfast, in fact.

'Well, there you are, you lucky girl,' said Diana happily. 'Now, is there anything else we can do for you or are you all right?'

'No, I'm perfectly fine. I'll just sit here and enjoy until you finish!' I grinned sleepily across at Diana again, knowing that she was on a mission from the angels to get through the material and that the odd visit from thirteen-foot energies, from we don't know where, would not deter her. It was absolutely true: I was quite content just to sit there for several more minutes with my eyes closed and just 'enjoy'. No further words can describe what I felt – but a daily dose of that feeling, straight into my very soul, would go down very well indeed. When the group broke for lunch I discovered to whom the Irish voice belonged as Joanne Maguire came dashing across the room in a somewhat diffident way. Dashing diffidently is a skill in itself.

'I wonder, would you mind . . . ? I mean, would you like to know . . . ? I mean, if it doesn't upset you and I'm not interfering . . . I think there's someone who wants to talk to you still here,' she said. Now where had I heard that before?

'Look, just sit down and please tell me – no, wait a minute, I want to write down everything you say.' I was so excited because it could only be Ian who had chosen yet another Irish voice to speak to me – significantly, seven years had elapsed since the last young Irishwoman had spoken for him in south-west England, and now here we were in south-west France. I could hardly wait.

Joanne and I did not know anything about each other at the time, as the course had not been going for very long. There was certainly no way that she could have known about Ian, whose first words to me were, surprisingly, 'Say happy birthday to Derek.' I am not even certain if it is correct to put speech marks around a dead man's speech channelled through a third party. What an odd concept.

I mentioned earlier that Ian was to have a strange relationship with my new friends Anne and Derek in France, even though they had never met. Here he was again, and it was indeed Derek's birthday. Even more bizarre, on the previous 1 April, which also happened to be Easter Day, I had thrown a surprise party for him to celebrate the fact that he had recovered from a life-threatening illness. With the help of my wonderful neighbours, amidst much fun and laughter trestle tables and chairs had been set out for fifty-five people. I loved such times in our neighbourhood when we all joined together to contribute to a dinner or other celebration; everyone was particularly happy on this occasion, as we were so pleased that Derek was better. I was flattered when I heard Joe, who helped in the garden and must have overheard my request to the sky for a sunny day to follow, say, 'But Susan, you are our sunshine!' How kind of him to say something so sweet. This retired gentleman is also very much in touch with nature and once told me that he hugs trees when he has a sore back. What amazing people one meets in the most unlikely places.

It was a real pleasure shared by us all to prepare for the day ahead. I decided that the tables looked so pretty after all our work that I took a photograph of the prepared and seemingly empty room. The next day I escorted the suitably surprised Derek, as guest of honour, into the dining room to select his seat. He chose one halfway down the table and settled in to enjoy a good day. When, a week later, I reproduced on my computer screen the photograph I had taken the night before the party, there on that very chair was a distinct presence. What is more, there appeared to be another form sitting behind Derek's chair on the small wicker settee. Derek, Anne and I were speechless.

'It must be my guardian angel on the chair, and that'll be Ian sitting behind,' said the normally sceptical and very sensible Derek when he found his voice. Now it was Anne's and my turn to look at each other in amazement. Later I heard Anne talking to her daughter, Alex, in England on the phone: 'Yes, of course she scares us half to death most of the time – but we love her anyway!' Can't think who she was referring to.

Therefore, one year later, Ian was quite correct to wish Derek a happy birthday and he appeared to be proving our previous year's assumption right – he had been there and had managed to get himself on to a photograph too. Joanne went on to tell me many more things that were obviously from Ian – he mentioned our daughter-in-law and new granddaughter by name. Niven had not found his soulmate until five years after his father's death; how wonderful to know that Ian has seen and approves his son's choice. He told me how proud he was of both our children, and also mentioned a blue car that meant nothing to me at the time. He said that he still had broad shoulders – I took that to mean that he was still supportive when I needed him. I jotted down several other things that were significant to me. Later that day, my son rang to tell me that he had just ordered a new blue car.

So here we were again, with Ian still saying he was around me – I never seemed to ask questions when this happened but was just so happy that he had chosen to speak when he did. This time he had introduced me to a new, very gifted and compassionate psychic healer. Joanne Maguire and I were to go on to share some very interesting and special healing moments together. Since that time I have seen her help many people in a humble, sensitive and quite incomparable way.

Later that day, when I had calmed down, another clairvoyant person in the class came to me and said, 'He says the
chocolates were his fault!' I immediately burst out laughing,
because it was Ian again, referring to a day shortly after he
had died when I was standing in front of the fire in our home
in Ireland, debating whether I should indulge myself with one
of the chocolates from the box I was holding. While I was
fighting this mental battle the whole box managed to do a
somersault into the back of the fireplace, with not an edible
piece to be saved. I automatically said, 'Thanks, Ian', as he
knew that I was always fighting the pounds and tried to
avoid sweets of any sort. Now here he was telling me that it
had indeed been his spirit that saved me from guilt again. It
was even more weird that I knew exactly what she was
talking about, as if he had entered our two minds at the same
time. This definitely does happen: I can be feeling the tell-tale
pressure in my ears when the telephone rings and Joanne on
the other end of the line, in a different country, will tell me
what Ian is saying to her for my information. It could just be
that he prefers chatting to pretty young women, of course.

Many other fascinating situations arose on this, my last
angel course before moving on yet again. The golden presence was hard to beat, but we all agreed that the wonderful
environment of this quiet corner of France added greatly to
the atmosphere. We had lots of warm, sunny days that
enabled us to do group work outside in the fresh air. Not
only did we feel angel energy, but we also felt that unicorns
were with the group. During some of the group meditations it
became apparent that the horses in the stable block, which
backed on to our excellent seminar room, often kicked the
walls and became quite vocal. Many students reported seeing
the mythical unicorns in their meditations. For reasons at
present known only to the Universe I often see Pegasus, my

winged horse friend, in dreams and meditations. If we look at medieval artwork we see that both of these equine creatures have appeared throughout history. We also noticed that the horses outside would immediately wander over to be part of whatever group exercises we were doing in the sunshine. Animals respond very quickly to additional environmental energy from whatever source.

It was when looking at photographs taken on this course that I first learned about energy spheres. The students had asked me to arrange a day out to visit some of the historic sites along the famous Dordogne valley. Little did we know that by the end of the day we would have photographic evidence of our spirit companions as we wandered around the medieval castles of the area. Much to my surprise, I actually enjoyed being a tour guide for the day as I guided the French bus driver from Cars Bleus in Eymet to pick up the angel students (what a lovely expression – much better than students of angels). The poor driver did not know what he was letting himself in for, but he was a great help and happy to change plan when the group decided that we needed to follow a whim and visit a local crystal importer. The proprietor thought that Christmas had arrived when twenty people tumbled in all ready to feel the energy of his huge, magnificent chunks of minerals from all over the world. Some of the smaller polished crystals were snapped up by the students, and those with large suitcases even managed to buy some big pieces of raw crystal. What an unexpected pleasure to find such a business on the back roads of the Dordogne valley.

I took along my usual digital camera, the one that had recorded Derek's angels, and generally snapped away as we toured the castle of Beynac. This site, allegedly dating back to Viking times, is a feudal fortress commanding impressive views over the Dordogne river. The castle is surrounded by a village with Gallo-Roman origins. There is a good chance that some of the English Plantagenet kings, Henry II and Richard the Lionheart, would have rested their horses here. Thus the castle, with buildings dating back to the seventh and eighth centuries, has seen a lot of history and harbours quite a few spirits from several dimensions. How do I know? I was touched by one.

I happened to notice Joanne standing transfixed in front of a small chapel in the main hall. The public are separated from the chapel by a wooden grille, to protect a very old fresco depicting Jesus and the Last Supper. As I went to stand beside her I could feel the energy bounce into my arm like electricity from Joanne's arm.

'What is it? What can you see?' I asked.

'Look! You must be able to see him – he's looking towards you,' she replied.

'No, I can't. I can feel the energy coming through you but I can see nothing,' I said, frustrated by my lack of clair-voyancy. I stretched my hand through the wooden bars to see if I could feel more energy coming from the direction in which Joanne was looking.

Suddenly I felt a sharp electric shock-type prick to my middle finger – a similar thing had happened some time earlier in Hawaii. 'Wow! What was that?' I asked as I jumped backwards. I turned to look at Joanne, who was nodding serenely at her source and whispering, 'Thank you.'

She told me that she had asked this old priest or medieval holy man to let me know that he was there. He certainly did a very good job, and I can still feel that amazing sensation of having been jolted with a small cattle prod on my middle finger.

The photographs that I took in the castle and later in an

old abbey were covered in white spheres of concentrated energy whenever we were in very spiritual areas. I have been told that this is the members of the spirit world trying to let us know that they are with us. They are warm and loving energies who are here for our protection, and take this form in order not to scare us. I have since identified such spheres in many areas of my life and I am sure you will, too, once you believe what you see on photographs. I have photographs of such spheres near a 'fairy well' and places of natural beauty where the nature spirits excel themselves. When I use my aura camera, photographs taken of the room also show this spirit interest in photographic energy work. I recently looked through an American website illustrating spiritual retreats, and at least a third of the photographs contained similar spirit spheres; they were definitely working with universal energy there.

As we walked through the magnificent buildings, accompanied by an excellent French tour guide, we asked her to give us time to 'feel' the energies inside. She was very polite and did not even suggest that she thought we were all mad. On the contrary, she was fascinated because she believed that she had Cathar forebears and wanted to know exactly what people were feeling from the ancient stone walls. The Cathars were a medieval Christian splinter group who believed in dualism – essentially, two Gods, one benign and one evil – and that man can only reach God by becoming aware of the divine origin of his own soul. The Cathar elite, known as *parfaits*, preached, amongst other things, absolute detachment from the material world. The Cathars were centred on south-west France and used many of the Dordogne castles and abbeys. Because of their failure to conform they were persecuted by the Pope and the French monarchy, and there was an infamous massacre of Cathar knights in 1244 at the hilltop fortress of Monségur. I really must find the time to go back and show the very patient and sympathetic tour guide some of the spirit spheres on my photographs that could just be the ancient spirits of her Cathar ancestors.

Our final stop was not, as I had wanted, the ancient abbey at Cadouin where I have had several interesting spiritual encounters, because it was unexpectedly closed. However, it was obviously another synchronicity of that special day because we visited instead the old abbey at St Avit de Senieur, where some fascinating things occurred. The site dates back to the Iron Age, when it was called Mont d'Auriac and served an earlier sacred function as a pagan temple; over the generations it became a stopping point for pilgrims *en route* to St Jacques de Compostela in Spain. Here we were privileged to be able to hold a group Om in the middle of the ancient aisle. While we were all wandering around feeling the energies once more, a Frenchman came up and asked me what we were doing. When I told him about our work with angels and healing he was very happy and asked if he could join in a group Mah (similar to an Om, and chanted to raise the energy). I have a photograph of this man hovering behind some of the group, so I know he was there, but, oddly, no one saw him leave or enter, and when we asked the ever-patient bus driver if he had seen the chap leave he answered, '*Quel homme?*' What man?

On the way home, as we were being driven along the tree-lined banks of the river, I did a guided meditation using the bus's microphone. As I finished, our driver leaned over to say that he had no idea what I had been saying but he had needed to be very careful not to fall asleep at the wheel. Even a Frenchman who could not understand English had been almost put into a trance by my words – now, where could I use this to my advantage?

On one of our rare days free from study a number of the students decided to come to my home for a walk in the garden. Joanne was one of the group, and as she walked into my office she saw Ian immediately.

'He's here, and he wants to talk,' she told me.

'In that case hang on a minute,' I said, and rushed off to fetch something that I had left untouched for several years in the drawer beside my bed. It was a strong plastic packet that contained Ian's medals and the singed banknotes that had been on his body when he died. I placed the packet, folded in two, on Joanne's outstretched palm. When holding this package in the early weeks after Ian's death I had often felt an inner calm, and I felt it would perhaps help her to tune in at a higher level now.

As she spoke to Ian's spirit I could feel the sparkling energy in the air around us both. She said, 'He says you must be able to see by now.'

'I just can't,' I whispered, my voice choked with emotion.

'Concentrate,' Joanne said gently. 'He says he wishes he could hold you, and he can't believe that you kept that burnt cash so long without spending it.'

No matter how hard I tried I could not see, but I knew there was another presence in the room with us and it felt very good indeed. Also, as I looked at the packet sitting on Joanne's hand it suddenly flipped open unaided. It actually appeared as if the plastic casing had a life of its own and was breathing. I took it into my hands to feel the warmth of this supposedly inanimate object, and watched Joanne speaking softly to what she could see in front of her and was obviously trying to coax towards her.

'Come on, come closer,' she whispered as if to a small child or animal, until she suddenly burst into laughter.

'What is it?' I asked, bemused.

She pulled a wry face and waved her arms in front of her in an almost perfect impersonation of a familiar mannerism of Ian's, and coincidentally of my daughter's. 'He says he's not really too sure about all that there spiritual stuff!' The accent was also Ian's, and I could easily imagine him saying just that while he was alive.

I decided I needed to ask a question that had often occurred to me. 'Ask him why he's still here, and have I in some way prevented him from going to peace in his death?' I then held my breath as Joanne waited and listened to the answer.

'He's saying he did pass over and was met by a woman – but he's been given a special dispensation to stay for a while. There are things you have to do.'

'What things?'

'He's showing me an old painting – do you remember? Of a man at a desk writing?'

I did indeed. He had bought it for a surprise and hung it on the wall above my desk in Ireland while I was writing up my PhD thesis. The only problem was that I had not noticed it for several days, and the 'surprise' went a bit flat. It became a source of teasing about my lack of observation when I am writing.

'Well, he says you have something important to write now and should get on with it!'

Amazing how, even from the grave (if he had one, which he doesn't), he is still bossing me about. Funnily enough I don't mind at all. This is the book that I hope he approves of. I feel it is important for him, because he did believe in an afterlife and would have wanted to be able to reassure those suffering or near death that good things are still to come. The pain of leaving our loved ones appears to be compensated for as we pass over. The soul really does continue, and its power can be used for the good of the Universe. It is important to have no regrets in our journey forward; although I knew that I had no regrets about our life together, I had not always been sure that I had made the right decisions at the time of Ian's death. I now knew that he would have approved of the memorial trips and fun things that we did with our friends as a family to commemorate his death and celebrate his life.

After that session in my office with Joanne I spent a few hours ringing both my children to ask them if they had seen the painting that their dad had spoken about. Having moved house twice in the interim, I thought there was a risk that I might have given it away or left it with Nicola or Niven. No, they had not seen it – and no wonder, because when I raised my head from my desk once more there it was, hanging exactly where I had hung it five years before in my office in France. Déjà vu?

The final fascinating experience with the students on the course in Bergerac happened in the local health food store in the old town. I had visited this shop on several occasions, to buy joss sticks and my crystal pendulum used for dowsing. I had noticed that the owner had installed a set of crystal singing bowls similar to the one owned by the Scottish colleague that I had first seen on the course in Somerset the previous year. Little did I know just how special Denis, this shopkeeper, was. One day a group of students were visiting the store, searching for interesting foods, crystals and so on, when I asked Denis if he would give us a demonstration of the singing bowls. He charmingly agreed and invited each person to stand in front of the row of different-sized bowls. Apparently each bowl corresponds to one of the body's chakras, and the sound that each makes interacts at a different pitch according to the individual's energetic state. In other words, it diagnoses whether body or energy flow is in a state of balance or not. It was wonderful to watch as this gifted man turned his back on the person being 'tested' and made a sound with each bowl. The sound emanating from the crystal almost makes the person go into a trance-like state, and the rest of the group stood close by in case any swaying body should fall. Luckily this did not happen, and everyone was very happy with their diagnosis. As he was finishing, Joanne whispered to me that he was actually working with his dead grandfather, whose spirit she could see standing beside him as he worked.

I translated this comment to Denis, who smiled and said, '*Ah oui, toujours!*' Ah yes, always.

Joanne went on to say that the old man was saying that his grandson talked a lot – in her words, he was 'an ole blether'.

Denis responded with a chuckle and said, in that very matter-of-fact manner that I have heard such gifted people so often use when speaking about the spirit world, 'He always says that.' He continued to talk to me in French and then said something quite astounding as he pointed to Joanne. '*Elle est un ange, tu sais?*' You know that she is an angel?

I assumed he was referring to her lovely personality and said, 'Oh yes, I know she's very nice!'

'*Mais non, tu comprends pas – elle* EST *un ange!*' But you don't understand – she really *is* an angel.

What does one say to that? Those people who have been helped by Joanne Maguire, either in a clairvoyant reading as a medium, or with her spiritual healing skills or her complementary therapies in acupuncture or reflexology, may well agree.

Later in the week I paid my final visit to the store with some students who were on their way home via the train station in Bergerac – of course, they had to have a quick stop for another 'go' with the bowls. One man was quite astounded by Denis's second diagnosis as he turned to me after playing all the different sounds.

'But what has happened to his heart chakra this week?' demanded Denis.

'What do you mean?'

'It is like a *crise cardiaque*,' a heart attack. 'Something amazing has changed the energy coming from his heart area.'

The rest of the group giggled in a conspiratorial way. We all knew that he had in fact fallen in love during the course, and it had been a pleasure for us all to see two people happy in each other's company. Someone joked that perhaps everyone should take their lovers into the shop to see if their hearts were similarly affected. Who would have thought that some lumps of crystal, in the right hands, could be so discerning?

I went on to read about crystals in more depth, and braved a day's course in French about using crystals as healing tools. My friend Michael's partner, Raymond, a man of special gifts, came with me. He had been a gemmologist many years before and had never lost his fascination with gems and minerals, in spite of now being involved at a very high level with worldwide information technology. We all seem to come back to natural things in the end. Raymond and I were very interested to see exactly how Jean-Marie, the course tutor, balanced people's chakras by placing crystals in appropriate places around or upon the body. In French the course was advertised as *Méthode pour Equilibrer et Harmoniser les Chakras par les Pierres et les Cristaux*. By pure chance again (or was it?) I had seen the course advertised while visiting the crystal workshop with Diana's angel group. Again I was amazed to meet so many French people from diverse backgrounds who were working as spiritual healers using the universal energy. Some spoke of God, others just spoke of energy, but I have no doubt they all accessed the same source to empower their clients. It was odd that Jean-Marie should choose the most sceptical member of the group, Raymond, to demonstrate the power of a three-crystal triangle. He asked Raymond to stand in the middle of three stones – rose quartz, amethyst and iron pyrites. As he asked him to turn from one direction to the other there was a definite change in my cool pal's facial expression. He said he had felt a real vibration through his whole body, which was verified by a number of other students who had measured the power of his aura before and after the triangle session. Whatever happened, it certainly sent him back to his seat looking very relaxed. Raymond leaned over to me to share, I thought, his profound experience, but instead whispered discreetly in my ear, 'Is it time for aperitifs yet?'

14
Rediscovering Hopes and Dreams

As I returned to my memories to plan my writing I reflected upon all of the other books that had entered my life, in a similar way to people, at just the right time. These memories were usually linked with some journey or other that I happened to be on at the time. One of the books that profoundly influenced my own personal healing was picked up as I browsed around a second-hand book store in Juneau, Alaska during a cruise of the breathtaking Inside Passage from Vancouver. The book, by Deepak Chopra MD, was called *Quantum Healing*. Here at last I was able to read about the mind–body link from a respected physician and holistic medical healer. He is world renowned for combining physics and philosophy with the practical and the spiritual aspects of Eastern wisdom and Western science, with dynamic results. I have since bought many more copies of his excellent books and given them to young medical student friends. If it makes just one new medical doctor look at their personal practice in a holistic and balanced way I shall be happy.

On that same cruise I thrilled at the sight of majestic mountains and glaciers while kayaking in waters that would have been canoed by early settlers from Gold Rush days and the indigenous population of Inuit and Native Americans. It was possible to be part of nature and feel the awe-inspiring history all at once. Travelling alone, as I was, gave me a lot of time to study the behaviour of my mainly American fellow passengers. One sunny morning we were in Glacier Bay, a place of exceptional beauty with its enormous tidewater glaciers, floating ice-castles and freezing blue-green water. I was on the very top deck, trying hard not to keep saying, 'Wow' and 'Awesome!' to myself, when a group of women in the middle of the deck caught my eye. I assumed that perhaps they were getting some local knowledge and edged closer to share what they were all listening to so attentively.

'Well, I just made a little old hole in the middle of my suitcase and popped it right on in there so it kept its shape.'

'How clever!'

'What a good idea.'

I thought perhaps she had found some great fossil to smuggle home, but no. The women were actually listening to one of their number explain in great detail how she had packed her designer sunhat to bring along on the cruise. And all this was taking place in the middle of one of the Northern Hemisphere's most breathtaking miracles of nature, where a whale could pop up at any moment. It made me realise that, even when surrounded by nature at its most magnificent, unless we have learned to value the moment on a spiritual, soul-enhancing level it can be lost. Perhaps I was being rather too judgemental, but I felt sad and amazed that these women, who appeared to have everything that money could buy, were missing so much in this very special place. Money cannot buy appreciation and respect for nature and our Universe. That comes free for the learning.

I was grateful all over again to my parents for their guidance and to Ian for having shared his love of the wilderness with us. Knowing what to look for and how to value nature in the grand scheme of things is in itself therapeutic and a great comfort for heart and soul. It does not take great intellect or resources – one just needs to *be* there. Nature in the raw also helps us appreciate the miracle of being alive, without designer sunhats. The lifestyle there gave me an ambition to return one day to those isolated settlements in Alaska that can only be reached by sea or small plane and really spend time in the wilderness. Another dream to fulfil.

A new dream came from a chance encounter between my son and a kind, dynamic couple in the Ariège region of France, which led to a satisfying friendship and a new focus for my energies in the Pyrenees. Niven had escorted a group of University Air Squadron students on an expedition following in the footsteps of escaping shot-down aircrew from the Second World War. He rang me enthusiastically to say how much he had enjoyed the company of a couple called the Goodalls when they had arranged to guide his group over the mountains, and he felt sure we would like to meet each other. As usual, he was right.

As a result of my contacting Scott and Judy Goodall I have been privileged to meet some brave and resourceful people in recent years. Although both now past retirement age, Scott coordinates the British contingent of the annual 'walk' – *Le Chemin de la Liberté* – from France into Spain to commemorate the magnificent bravery of not only the Allied escapees but also their local guides. The veterans and survivors who come along to remember their colleagues, and to say thank you to the families of those homes who gave them shelter while risking their own lives, are a pleasure to meet. Once again French hospitality is much in evidence when wonderful spreads of local produce are provided to greet walkers who arrive from all over Europe and America to undertake a gruelling four-day hike over the mountains. I have not yet been brave enough to try the entire four days, but the ever-supportive Judy has attempted to train me over parts of the route on my various visits. I love this area of France with its Cathar history and friendly people.

My aim is to find a small bolt-hole in Seix, a pretty village in the foothills of the Pyrenees, where I can join the local walking club and be guided safely up into the mountains where I can really feel part of nature. Yet another dream to fulfil in the future, even if I have to contend with the family saying, 'Mum's buying a bit of Sex at last!'

I have whetted my appetite (for mountain walking, not sex – but who knows?) by completing the two-day hike at the other end of the Pyrenees, organised by the Belgian Comète Line group in liaison with the local Basque Spanish support-ers, yet another enthusiastic group of people who take time and effort to commemorate the sacrifice made by so many brave souls sixty years ago. The whole occasion is marked by fun and laughter (at least from those who have breath to laugh while trudging up mountainsides) interspersed with heartfelt moments of commemorative silence. Some of the Basque walkers are remembering whole families wiped out during their bid to help Allied servicemen find their way to freedom.

Knowing that such people have suffered and coped val-iantly over the intervening years gives hope to many others who lose loved ones. For me, the inspiration of eighty-year-old Paul from the Ariège, one of the original guides, is hard to beat. I followed in his footsteps on my last two-day hike, and marvelled at the fitness level of this grand old gentleman. During the war he was imprisoned for his efforts to guide Allied airmen safely through these mountains that must be treated with respect if you are to survive. It clearly illustrates that life is what you make it, without bearing grudges and looking too much into the past to apportion blame. We all have choices in the here and now.

American walkers arrive to tread in the footsteps of their relatives who received help from local safe houses and to show their appreciation to the families who receive them so graciously. My favourite part is wading across the Bidasoa river, the demarcation line between France and Spain, at the end of day one. Being somewhat vertically challenged I had dreaded the first crossing, having spoken with a six-foot-tall, eighty-year-old veteran who assured me that when he had crossed as a young airman the water had been up to his chest. But he either crossed in heavy rain or enjoyed teasing, because I was relieved to find it just a comfortable thigh height. Scott, however, managed to make it look much more exciting, with a Union Jack strapped to his walking pole. No one commented on the fact that he lost the flag halfway over – we were all too busy munching freshly barbecued sardines and downing local wine generously provided on the far bank that was the wartime 'safe shore' of Spain. There are some great characters in this world who quietly get on with their important contributions to many lives other than their own.

Some characters of this kind came to join me in France for a mini angel-class reunion one September after the Somerset course. We set out with the idea of just getting together to have fun and meditate and soak up the French life. As usual with good ideas, it spiralled and ended up including a day workshop for my local friends who had continually asked me what I got up to on my angel courses. So it was that Heike from London, Marie-Louise, Sandra and Margaret from Scotland, and French-born Martine with her English husband Paul arrived to stay just as the local *vendange*, the grape harvest, was beginning to fill the air with its pungent, fruity aroma. My friends Drew and Silvie arrived slightly later, but in time to fall in love with the area and decide to live there too.

The most evocative memory of that time, for me, was the building of the Indian medicine wheel – a stone circle – in my garden. The idea evolved from my conversations with Sandra, an expert on Native American spirituality. She is also very in tune with ancient Mayan calendars from South America and has a marvellous understanding of the natural cycles of time as interpreted by Mayan visionaries – yet more ideas and concepts that I enjoyed learning about. Before she arrived she had asked me to choose a spot in the garden that I thought would be suitable for a large circle of natural stones, but not to tell her where it was. As I wandered about the comforting garden that I had developed from the original orchard and pine trees, at a particular moment I just knew that the ground under my feet, in a clearing amongst the tall, pungent pines, felt right. Just to check, I tried my amethyst pendulum over the spot and it swung happily round in circles, signifying a 'yes' to me.

When three of the girls went out to construct the circle I remained in the house, waiting to see which spot they would home in on. Sure enough, they gathered in a huddle over the very spot my pendulum had agreed with. Now in such a large garden that was amazing, and I was delighted. I can see them now, scurrying around heaving massive boulders of local stone towards the selected piece of ground. A compass is usually used to mark north, south, east and west, but with their inherent feel for the land they did not seem to need one. A central stone would be the power point of the circle or spirit stone, and the four main geographical directions emanating from it would also represent the elements of earth, air, fire and water. Each stone in a circle of this type represents something in one's life. In the months to come this stone circle was to be my sacred area of peace for meditation and reflection. The fact that it was situated amongst the trees, with views over plum orchards and rolling farmland, gave me a feeling of being at one with nature. I am very grateful to have been allowed to use this space for a while.

On the final night of our stay together we held a ceremony to bless the wheel of stones and thank everyone who had helped to make our impromptu week special. A bonfire was lit at the edge of the garden behind the stone circle, the wine was chilled to await our final supper together, and the food was prepared by the ever-helpful Maggie who seems to conjure scrumptious goodies from thin air. Her husband Barry, familiarly known as Bazza, was also there, throwing himself enthusiastically into the spirit of the day by wearing an Indian bhindi on his forehead. Michael and Raymond, together with Drew and Silvie, joined the rest of the group to help recite some beautiful words from I know not where. I was a little thrown to be told that I must stand in the middle at the spirit stone and start everything off with a few words – this was yet another occasion when I needed to call upon my inner self, higher self, the Universe and the stars above to help me. As I gulped and looked upwards I saw that immediately above me was a large and beautiful shining star surrounded by a constellation of smaller ones.

'Oh!' I gasped. 'What's that?'

'It's Andromeda,' volunteered Raymond the astronomer, from his position at the Western Stone. We had created candle-lit paths from the house to the wheel, and everyone had positioned themselves holding candles around the edge of the circle. It made a very pretty, romantic sight.

'Thank you – it couldn't be more perfect,' I said as emotion started to choke me.

How wonderful that so many good friends were humouring my whims yet again. The energy could be felt from the earth and in the air. There was a tangible presence of goodness and beauty, mingled with incense and natural herbs, in the atmosphere. My words, when they eventually came, were mostly of thanks, I seem to remember, but they were followed by the most soul-stirring drumming from Sandra's bodhran. The air was really beginning to pulsate now, and I could feel my soul starting to build more dreams for the future. It was certainly an evening to remember. As we walked away from the medicine wheel towards the house Michael slipped his arm around my shoulders.

'Well, darling,' he whispered, 'the neighbours will surely burn you now!'

My new dream (or was it Ian's?) of making a small contribution by writing again was accelerated a year later in Arcachon, a pretty little coastal town south of Bordeaux. I had decided to rent out my house for the summer with the vague idea of using the income to travel for a few months and gather material for a new book. But things did not work out quite to plan – I spent so much money and effort preparing the house for rental that travel seemed unlikely. Nevertheless I enjoyed my time in a hotel on the coast so much that I decided I could live near the sea again. It was there in the Novotel, nestled above the pine-clad dunes, that I met a manager who knew the secret of recruiting efficient, friendly staff. I commented on the welcoming smiles of everyone employed at this hotel and was delighted by his reply.

'Thank you, *madame*,' said Monsieur Vielfaure. 'I choose people for their bright and friendly personalities rather than their skills. I can train them to work well, but I cannot train them to smile or to like their fellow men.' It certainly works, and as a single traveller I was very pleased to feel the warmth of their welcome.

It was in the health spa attached to this hotel that I met a very special healer who does splendid relaxing massage treatment sessions with the help of an angel or two. Aline uses acupressure and her own mode of energy healing to find blockages in the client's body and free up the meridians to allow the body (and soul) to feel lighter and freer. As she worked on me by skilfully applying pressure on to specific areas along my meridians or energy lines I became aware of at least two other energy fields in the room. I could plainly see the wonderful bright aura around her head and shoulders, and there was also a brightness coming from two other body-like shapes behind her. Yes, she did indeed believe in and work with angel energy, she told me when I tentatively asked the question. She was surprised that I had spoken about it, as she usually keeps this special help for her work a closely guarded secret in case anyone thinks she is a little bizarre. To say that I floated out of her treatment room would be an understatement. It is a very relaxing and profound experience when you find a therapist like that who works with her heart and soul, by accessing other energy from the Universe to help her clients. This form of healing goes far deeper than the muscles or skin being massaged, and is carried out with real love from above. How good to know that there are so many excellent thera-pists out there who work with healing energy in their own quiet way. When you have been touched in this way, you will know it. Unfortunately there are bluffers and charlatans in all professions, and you need to be discerning when accepting a massage or treatment. Make sure that you feel right in the environment and with the therapist; trust your intuition at all times.

Protecting oneself from negative energy is an important habit to adopt when you come into regular contact with the general public. I mentally encase myself with protective energy from the angels or the Universe if I am going to be in close contact with other people, especially in crowded places. We can often arrive home after a day in a busy office, perhaps with a journey on a crowded train afterwards, feeling sticky and drained. The stickiness is caused not just by heat; it can also be the result of other people's heavy energy being transmitted from their aura to yours, either on touching or just passing in a small space. Sometimes this transmission can be energising, of course, but if lots of unhappy or depressed people have been in your space you will probably have absorbed some of these feelings too. The latest aura imaging technology makes it possible physically to see this interchange of energy between living organisms of all kinds. My advice is to visualise a beautiful protective golden ball all around your body before you leave the house each day; you will return home less tired and fresher than before. I also say thank you at the end of each day for this protection from our world of universal energy.

It was during that earlier visit to the hotel in Arcachon that I realised I could live a simpler life without a large garden and a swimming pool to look after. In fact, I fantasised that I would like to live in a hotel, where I could devote more time to working with healing and angel groups of people around the world and to my writing. The time I had devoted to self-indulgent gardening and entertaining in France had started to make me feel guilty. Now was the moment to make a move, or else I would sit and vegetate nicely in my sun-drenched garden, enjoying the company of my truly good friends there; I knew that there were things to do. Once more, synchronicity showed me the next step. A young man who rented my house for two weeks decided that he would quite like to buy it and have his own French lifestyle. I am not sure which of the two of us was the more surprised when I said I would sell my haven of peace.

I set off to visit my friend June in Spain one more time and we thought back to when she had been newly widowed two years before. We had been walking along a quiet beach with only very few buildings and some natural parkland nearby. When we stopped to sip a glass of chilled white wine in a little *chiringuito* – a rustic beach bar – called Heaven we could see Morocco across the blue sea. 'This can't be bad,' we had said as we sat with our feet in the warm sand. 'If this is heaven, then we are pretty close to our men, and the sun and wine seem a pleasant enough way to suffer our loss.' It is difficult to believe that this particular spot is on the crowded 'costas' at all, because it is so peaceful and surrounded by wildlife. I had remarked that I would like to be in these parts if ever I considered moving to Spain. Remarkably an apartment that suited my needs perfectly did become available, at just the right time, not far from this quiet corner of the coast. So there I was, as usual finding the jigsaw pieces of my life fitting together much more quickly than I had anticipated. I had never considered being an apartment dweller until my stay at that friendly Novotel in Arcachon. All part of life's rich tapestry, perhaps, but I do believe that everyone who crosses our path has something to offer as part of our ever-growing jigsaw if we keep our eyes open. It would be a shame not even to start putting the pieces together by leaving everything in the box.

I went back to France to complete the sale of my house there, clear out the junk accumulated over the years and move on with very little apart from the artwork and personal effects. I had decided it was time to leave behind all my past life's baggage, mental and physical. As ever, my circle of friends and family muscled in to help to save me from a nervous breakdown. Earlier in the year my niece Rachel and her husband Keith had arrived in France to become farmers, and it was great for them to be able to use me as an access point to the local community and – more importantly – help me with my packing. It all seemed such a rush, but that is the way I do things: spontaneity works well for me. Nothing was finalised either for the sale in France or the purchase in Spain until the very last week before I planned to move, and I did end up feeling rather stressed. To rescue me I was sent two more angelic helpers in the form of Joanne from Belfast and my daughter Nicola from London, who found a few days to come over and help me empty my cupboards for the *vide-grenier* – literally 'attic emptying', equivalent to a garage sale in English. The bonus of having a resident clairvoyant and spiritual healer was that Nicola and I received one of the most amazing healings ever.

Joanne felt that she had been guided to come over to help me relax before this important life change and I was de-lighted to accept a spiritual healing combined with some reflexology. We prepared my sitting room, which was start-ing to fill with packing cases, by lighting candles and burning joss sticks to clear the air of all negativity. The fact that this house had always felt very light and full of love had made it a shrine to positive thinking. I had also commissioned a local stained-glass artist, Jenny Weller, to create two stained-glass windows for my terrace doors. Using hand-blown glass, just as in medieval church windows, Jenny had designed them beautifully to depict many aspects of my life and they let a living picture of ever-changing light enter the room at dif-ferent times of day. They made the house feel very special for me, with their Pegasus image and a phoenix discreetly tucked in amongst the wings, all in subtle colours like a painting in glass and lead. They would accompany the ever-present crystals to my new life in Spain.

As I lay on my couch Joanne worked around my aura with

her hands, gently regenerating the energy of my chakras which had got very low after all the rushing around and last-minute planning. We all share our energy with others in our daily lives, and it can become depleted unless we spend time reactivating our own batteries. As Joanne worked I could feel an enormous energy in the room and had a vision of a Native American – an old Indian woman. This could well have been my imagination, cynics will say, but I know that I could not have invented the tremendous feelings of relaxation and an almost cosmic love that surrounded me. I was just wondering how Joanne was managing to get my solar plexus area to feel so gently massaged when I suddenly became aware of her rubbing her hands together on the other side of the room from where I was lying. She wasn't anywhere near me – so who or what was pressing my midriff in such a comforting fashion? I had no idea, so when I eventually opened my eyes to see Joanne sitting smiling gently on the other settee I asked her what on earth I had felt.

'I just asked *them* to take over,' she said, 'and I could also see your spirit guide in the room – you know, your Indian Medicine Woman.' So that is who it was.

I also asked Joanne if she had felt another energy with us. We decided to draw our separate impressions of what we had felt or, in Joanne's case, 'seen'. Curiously, we both drew a tall, cloaked figure with a large triangular shape on his head and large eyes. She then asked me to say who I thought this guide would be, and I replied with the first thing that came into my head: 'Metatron.' Trust your intuition, the healing world says.

'Yes,' said Joanne ecstatically. 'I knew you were getting more psychic.'

I had no idea who this being was, but I looked the name up in several books and on websites and then rang Diana

Cooper for a double check. Among his various important roles Metatron is the archangel responsible for the eternal archives and the chief recording angel, and I am honoured that he chose to share an aspect of his energy with us. How appropriate that his energy was felt just when I was starting to write a book suggested by someone in the spirit world. Metatron is mentioned in many sacred texts and in the Book of Genesis in the Bible. I am not in the habit of reading the Bible or any other religious text except when something affects my life in this way, but I have never let go of the idea of a loving God or almighty power that helps us in our everyday lives.

Many Christians think clairvoyance and spiritual healing go against the teachings of God. I have never understood this viewpoint, because a truly spiritual healer with clairvoyant gifts is in fact not calling up the dead but working with the living for their better health. The knowledge that angels and spirits from the other dimension call to clairvoyants to help them give comfort to the sick and the grieving is good enough for me. I have seen grief counselling go on for many years with bereaved people unable to come to terms with the death of their loved ones, yet in many cases one or two sessions with a gifted and sensitive medium or clairvoyant give great hope and reassurance.

The next day Joanne carried out a similar healing session with Nicola. We were due to go out to supper that evening and the wonderful atmosphere of peace and relaxation created by the two of them in the healing room – or should I say my crate-filled living room? – was so full of beautiful energy that they went on a little longer than anticipated. But I was happy for us to be late for supper when I saw the light shining from my daughter's beautiful eyes at the end of the session, as she sat there glowing with health and happiness.

Even more amazing was the spirit energy that they both carried with them to our supper date. Someone took a photograph of the three of us during the meal, and I was thrilled to see the familiar spirit sphere of energy above Nicola's head as she grimaced in her usual way at the thought of having her photograph taken. I don't know exactly what it was: one minute it was there and then it disappeared, and it looked very similar to all those other spheres that I had seen often on photographs around Joanne and had also observed around Diana's angel teaching group in Bergerac the year before.

I was just so grateful that Joanne and my daughter had become friends and that Nicola now knew that her mother had not been completely mad when I enthusiastically told my family about the joys of spiritual healing and my clairvoyant friend. Now, as I was moving on again, I could sense the different aspects of my old and new lives coming together in a productive and satisfying way. I had long since learned that when my ears felt pressure in them it was Ian talking or trying to convey a message to me. It may just have been that he was letting me know that I am still loved, but more than likely he was trying to motivate me into action. On one occasion in the previous year my ear was very painful and I stopped to ask myself why, if it was Ian communicating, I should feel such pain. The voice came into my head immediately, loud and clear: 'You need some pain before the good stuff. Talk to me while I'm listening – take love, take life, tell all, say it like it is, use your intuition, your wisdom and get rid of superstition by listening to your own inner wisdom and remove fear for ever. Look for the spheres: they're good energy, here to help.'

I wrote all of this down, at the time, and found my notes just in time to pack them for the move. I had dated them – 8

November 2003, the date of the Harmonic Concordance of planets, a total lunar eclipse on the night of the full moon. I realised once more that Ian has been with me to help complete this book, and I came to I feel him less as the final lines were being written. I remember how much he liked the film in which Richard Dreyfuss played a dead pilot whose spirit does not move on until he knows his lover is happy again. Perhaps he is waiting for me to find a new love before he goes back to base for his well-earned rest; or perhaps he will always have the potential to visit when I need him. Perhaps he knows of my new sense of peace verging on serenity.

Just as I finished writing those notes that I presumed to be from Ian and my higher self, the telephone rang in the house in France. Joanne, who had since returned home to Belfast, had been prompted by simultaneous messages from Ian to contact me. She told me that he had wanted me to get the word 'mediator'. I had not managed to hear it, so there was the evidence I needed: it had been his words to me. He felt mediation would be one of my new jobs, just as he had often used me to mediate while he was alive.

As Joanne and I had this telephone conversation my niece Rachel arrived to say hello, and I motioned for her to have a seat until I had finished. Joanne then said that Ian was telling her that he was actually standing at my shoulder as I had been writing the words down, and he was still there. I replied that I thought I could feel the customary tingles in my spine and suddenly the door behind me flew open of its own accord; there was certainly no one there in the physical sense. I glanced across at Rachel to see that she had tears in her eyes and was looking across the room at me and the door, obviously very shaken. As I got off the phone she told me she felt 'all fuzzy and weird'. She had also seen an image of light standing behind me just as the door had swung open, although she did not tell me this until later, after she had shared her experience with her husband. Down-to-earth, well-balanced farmer Keith had no problems in accepting the account of what he also assumed to be either Ian or an angel in my house. He already knew that his father's spirit visited his mum on a regular basis. How does she know? She smells his pipe smoke.

I find that people in rural communities, who live and work with nature, can accept the other dimensions and their helping energy without the suspicion of city folks with their technology and plastic everythings that interfere with energy reception. Yes, it is shades of 'beam me up Scottie!' and how exciting is that? Later still, after the house move that had prompted all this had taken place, I was discussing the sensations experienced by both Rachel and myself with my friend Raymond, who has his own healing gifts. I was waxing lyrical as usual about the use of clairsentience (feeling spiritual energy), and stated that Rachel was obviously very sensitive to environmental energy and would be something special one day. 'Yeah,' said the laconic Raymond, 'she will. She'll be locked up – like her aunt!'

It is odd how one evolves with grief, through learning and perhaps a more objective view of life. By this I mean that as I grieved I felt I was not part of real life, that I had stepped off the world and was looking back on other people as they went about their daily lives. I had a sense of being a bystander for several years. Nothing could hurt me, or so I felt, and life problems became clearer and less threatening. If I thought about doing something, such as moving to France and now to Spain, I just got on and did it, without too much planning and preparation.

I do not really know why I suddenly decided that France

was not to be my final home after so many special things shared there. I had moved from Ireland when I heard a friend unthinkingly say that Sunday lunch at my home there was 'just like old times'. It had not been 'like old times' for me, nor could it ever be again. I now felt that 'being well settled' was not what was meant to happen next in my life's journey. I had loved the old-fashioned, peaceful life in the rolling hills of the Lot-et-Garonne and the only slightly more sophisticated Dordogne. I had appreciated learning to be valued as a person in my own right once more, and I had spent seven years learning a new language and adopting a culture that I had grown to love. I really had learned to be 'me' and not just half of 'us'. This was one of those statements I had made at the time of the publicity tour for the first book, without really thinking too much about it. In a long-term, loving relationship I had wholeheartedly become 'we' and 'us' and that concept had integrated itself into my psyche. While giving interviews in 1996 I had often opened my mouth before engaging my brain, but over recent years I hope I have gained more wisdom. We really do need to learn something new each day of our lives if we are not to become stale, complacent, arrogant or just prematurely old. I know I could have earned all of those labels at various times of my life. My move from France was part of my ambition to rock that stale, complacent old boat that I was in danger of never rocking again.

15
The Final Goodbye

More literal boats in the form of island-hopping ferries were to be shared with Joanne when I next travelled to Scotland to visit my son and his family. She had volunteered to come with me on my final private visit to the Mull of Kintyre, just before the tenth anniversary of Ian's death. For some reason I really wanted to see if there were more things that Ian needed to say to me at the place where he had physically left this earth for ever.

I had sold my French house and purchased my new home in Spain, with everything falling into place at the last moment just as I had known it would. I had been practising visualising successful conclusions and it worked well – probably because I was dealing with fair-minded people, but still with some divine guidance, I like to think. Even Maître Morton, the very stylish lady *notaire* in France, was amazed that a final official form arrived in the nick of time on the morning that I was due to hand over the keys and sign away my beautiful home. Considering that the purchaser was called Nick, that fitted quite nicely.

My good pals Michael and Raymond very kindly offered me their spare room in which to rest and recoup some energy before I finally set off to my new life, following the swallows south at last. It was difficult to leave the warm and easy friendship that I enjoyed in their home. Their beautiful Vizsla dog, Lily, looked as though she knew something I didn't as I finally walked out of the door.

The two-day drive to Spain left me feeling as I had done after my first move from Ireland to France, almost eight years before. I had come home once more, on yet another new path to new adventure. It was to be a very different life in my apartment with its view of Morocco over the Mediterranean. The fact that I was nearer to heaven, even though it was only a beach restaurant that served delicious fish, seemed a good move. I could happily walk a beach before breakfast again, only this time not the chilly pebbles of Northern Ireland but the warm sands of Spain. I could also shut my door behind me and go travelling without worrying about the garden and other things that needed constant maintenance. In my life I had lived in England, Ireland, France and Spain, and my journeying over the past ten years had taken me to Thailand, Hawaii and my favourite British Columbia, as well as out into the Universe where there is free travel for all. Now from Spain I could journey more easily, wherever I wished, since Malaga airport was close and several airlines operated from there.

So it was that I flew to Scotland to spend some happy days with Niven, Sheena and my two gorgeous grandchildren just two months after I had embarked on my new Spanish life. I then drove to Glasgow airport to meet Joanne from the Belfast flight, and together we drove north towards the Mull of Kintyre. This route to Argyll can either be done the long way round, by road, or more directly on local ferries. I love this magnificent area, with its mountain passes and rivers meandering through the glens to the lochs. Yes, Ian had really picked a great place to die.

The final ferry journey to the Mull was from Portavadie to Tarbert, and unfortunately the winter timetables meant that we had an hour or so to wait at the slipway in Portavadie. That really is all it is – a concrete slipway. As the grey, choppy waters lapped the sides of the ramp that stretched down into the depths of Loch Fyne we decided to pass the time by playing a meditation CD on the car radio. It was one of those meditations to activate your energy fields and help you to feel surrounded by a healing light. As the CD finished we turned to each other and said, 'Were you nudged?' I said I had felt my arm pushed quite hard from behind, and Joanne too had felt herself nudged in the arms. She then asked me if I had ever learned the name of my Indian medicine woman spirit guide.

I said, 'No, why?'

'Because she's sitting in the back of the car right now.'

'Ah well, in that case she must be a Chinook Indian. Right?'

'Right, because she's leaning forward at that response in a very positive way.'

I had brought along my new box of healing cards, designed and written by Carolyn Myss PhD, the American medical intuitive and healing counsellor, and offered a card to Joanne as I opened the explanatory booklet. I had already marked one of the pages a few days earlier. Joanne held up the very card of the page that I had marked; it was card number 45, which reads:

May all creation dance for joy within you
All you want to do today is love being alive
Even if it's the hardest thing you've ever done.
Appreciate the sounds, sights and sensations of your
    life
Friends, books, ideas, sleep. . . .
Just enjoy.

A good philosophy, but for me the significant factor was that the booklet stated that it came from a Chinook Indian prayer. It had taken almost ten years for the word 'Chinook' to have a more positive meaning, and now we were on our way to the site of the Chinook helicopter crash on the southernmost point of the Mull of Kintyre.

In recent years I had started to look for links in many areas of my life and this journey was a crossroads linking all that I had researched and thought about, and my meditations that had given me inner strength to go forward on a more spiritual path. I felt that I had my feet firmly grounded from the balance of my old life and from the sense of humour of friends and family that had always been a comforting stabiliser. I had made many notes over the years recording my thoughts and observations; even my dreams were recorded as I looked for patterns and a deeper understanding of life's journey.

As we travelled I thought about some of my notes, which I had recently been re-reading, about people peeping through holes in walls and doors. On one of my sitting and observing days in Spain, I had watched people as they walked casually past a hoarding separating some building work from the pavement. Almost everyone who passed had to stop and peer through a small hole cut into the otherwise opaque hoarding. We *have* to look, don't we? Is it because we can look without becoming involved, because we really want to be a fly on the wall? This is why reality television programmes are so popular, I am sure. We can observe and experience, vicariously, without becoming involved – in fact with no interaction involving ourselves at all. This is fine for a time, unless it turns into a 'hands off' attitude to life in general. The human animal was not meant to be an isolated individual. Society is built on interpersonal interactions, and disintegrates when we operate the Peeping Tom syndrome and do not get involved. There can be no doubt that successful interactions must come from a background of personal knowledge. Everyone we meet has something to teach us.

How well do we know ourselves? Do we like ourselves? Do we enjoy spending much time with ourselves, or are we operating a hole-in-the-wall policy to life? Alternatively, are we jumping through that hole to join groups without really knowing why? If someone looks back through that hole, do we offer a friendly greeting or jump back in shock and hope that they have not seen us? It is not surprising that depression is the fastest-growing problem in our increasingly anonymous society. Learning about ourselves is the first step to learning about others. Learning about the other dimensions of our life and the world contributes even more to our fuller understanding of any situation. I realised that I was happy to jump through all those holes and enjoy whatever whichever dimension had to share with me, despite the fact that I had been accused of a morbid curiosity because of my work with psychics and angel healers. As Joanne and I admired the peaceful beauty of a land that was so similar to where Ian and I had lived and loved, I told her of these thoughts. We were discussing her PhD studies into all manner of complementary therapies for cancer patients. I was amazed that there is such a plethora of research material illustrating the therapeutic effects of energy healing and touch for cancer patients; it fitted my personal research over the previous ten years. I knew now that anything that reminds us that we are capable of taking control of our own destiny with renewed passion, and that we can call on assistance from within and beyond ourselves, is good. I knew that we were indeed on the right track, and that the spiritual and physical tracks can be complementary. I realised that I had come to see the intrinsic connection of everything on earth and beyond as one. When it is a person's time to die, and usually not before, they do indeed pass on to another dimension. There is a higher energy than us, and the soul continues. We rarely die before our time, hard as it seems to those who are left behind to continue with their life contracts; there is ample proof of this, albeit intangible, in the worldwide respected literature. The well-trodden track to visit someone who can let a relative know their deceased loved one is at peace is rarely discussed, but it gives enormous comfort to thousands very quickly.

As we approached the single-track road at the end of the Mull we felt a real excitement, since this was my first visit for several years. It was a gloriously sunny day, with blue skies and a bitter wind blowing off the Irish Sea. We parked at the top of the hill and trekked down across the heather-clad hillside, to the cairn which had been built by a local man called Duncan Watson, to commemorate all twenty-nine who died there. We had not planned to do anything there other than sit and see what happened. Joanne knew little about the crash as she had been only nineteen at the time and it had not featured in her own life at all. I suggested to her that we sit roughly where I thought Ian's body had been found, above the cairn looking across the sea to County Antrim in Ireland. It was not long before Joanne was told to move up a bit: he was there, and telling us we were sitting in the wrong place. Typical!

So it was that on 23 March 2004, almost ten years after the fatal crash, I found myself listening to Joanne Maguire from Belfast speaking words from another dimension. I just sat beside her and took notes as she listened and saw. Once again, as in the castle in France, I could feel the electrical shivers come from her arm towards mine, only this time I saw something as well. I could actually see energy bouncing around in front of us against the backdrop of an icy-cold blue sea. I will reproduce some of my notes here, though without personal names to respect people's privacy. As we sat down I had started to see and feel a misty aura over the whole mountainside, but nothing could have prepared me for what was to happen next.

'Oh yes, I see,' said Joanne. 'They're telling me that they all walked up out of here together. Their souls left as a group – look.' As she spoke I had a pure image of a body of spirits walking up the hill together as though they were floating upwards. The emotional energy around us was magical, and almost exciting in a very sad way. I felt strangely elated and as though I were back on the day of the crash, and yet the air was pure and the sun-filled sky belied the misty evening of ten years before. Because of the blue sky I think I was able to see the shapes of figures, almost like a hologram against the sky. Joanne was already speaking as I was trying to focus even more on what I was seeing. I wrote the words down just as she spoke them; the italics depict voices that she reported directly from spirit:

'I don't know what that is doing here,' she said to me. 'A wee puppy dog spirit is running around my feet – how odd.'

'The devil didn't take us, ma girl,' she repeated in a broad Irish accent that was different from her own Belfast lilt.

'Oh, I can't quite get this name but I have the phonetic sound of it – yes, and there's a piano he's showing me very proudly. He sounds so proud,' she said.

'I can hear a violin playing here. I wonder what that means.'

As she spoke I could almost see the scenes that were being relayed to Joanne.

'Someone's dad was an old football player. He's showing

me this memory of an old leather ball and a man in old-fashioned kit for some reason.'

'Ach, give my head peace,' said Joanne in her own Irish accent. 'There's someone talking very quickly. I can't get what he's saying – very excited – odd – it's an English accent. He says, *'Fuck 'em the government.'* There were, of course, soldiers and aircrew and members of the security services from England in the helicopter as well as the contingent of Northern Irish police officers. I had not explained this to her before we arrived.

She continued to listen now with a smile on her face as she felt the emotion of the next voice to come to her.

'Passing over was much nicer than he imagined – it was a wonderful experience as he rose up – I can feel his happiness – nothing could have prepared him for the euphoric feeling as he died. Oh, I can't make it out – he's showing me a small khaki green suitcase-shaped box. He's pointing and saying it was faulty, over and over. I can't see what it is.' This could have referred to whatever was wrong with the helicopter that contributed to the crash, which remains an enigma to this day.

As Joanne continued I wished I also had someone with technical expertise there to ask appropriate questions. She continued to relate statements from a variety of individuals who all wanted to have their say. There were too many to report here, but the warmth and character of the many different personalities came through clearly, as though they had been waiting to chat for a long time. I felt honoured that they had chosen to come through the veil to talk to us so freely.

'*Ask my wife did she ever see a mist inside the house,*' someone requested in a very keen way. He had been trying to let his wife know that he was with her for comfort, and this was his chance to reinforce the message.

Then it was Ian's turn. I had been thinking that he was there as a sort of host to bring the other spirits forward. Oddly, I had not minded that he waited until last – just as though I could feel him with me, hosting a party, in the old days.

'*I feel real peace and contentment now,*' he said through Joanne, and then a miraculous thing happened: I actually heard his voice myself at the same time as Joanne did. He asked me whether I was going to join him: '*Are you ready to come over yet?*' I heard the voice in my head just before Joanne spoke the same words aloud.

Through my shock I replied, 'No, there are things still to do. . . .' How amazing and wonderful that I knew my answer so quickly and surely; just a few years before it might have been a very different answer.

'*Atta girl – too right – big stuff ahead – all your life training is coming in now. Yes, you were right. My last words were, "Oh fuck."*' Joanne was now chuckling again as she relayed these words, so typical of Ian. She could not know that the children and I had often speculated on what his last words would have been. We were not far off the mark.

His granny had apparently met him when he went over. Previously, he had just told us it was a woman; now we knew who it was.

'*Remember, actions speak louder than words.*'

'*You need proof – you need evidence.*' I would later discover what he meant when I started recording the presence of spirits on film.

'*You always were weird, Susan.*' Still the same lovely teasing humour – OK, so it may be true as well as funny.

At this point Joanne walked away across the heather and I experienced that wonderful glowing prickly feeling all over. My face felt as though it were being warmed by kisses, in spite of the freezing wind blowing in from the sea. It was all right, I knew – Ian was at peace at last and had told us so. I was overjoyed that I had actually received some of his messages directly at the same time as Joanne – my psychic skills were growing, and I was as happy about that knowledge as I was at hearing them from Ian for the first time. I now had proof that using our intuition is something of which we are all capable once we go past our concrete, society-programmed reactions to outside phenomena. As to how I 'got' the messages on this occasion, it was a voice that came into my head and a real 'knowing'. In previous 'communications' I had 'felt' or 'known the message'. It may sound odd, but that is the best description I can give.

As she was receiving messages on the heather I had been watching Joanne, who had been holding her hands up in front as if she were gripping something. I had at first thought that perhaps it was one of the pilots trying to pull up the controls but, as an expert kindly pointed out later, Chinook controls are not like that. In hindsight I reckon it could well have been someone sitting with their hands gripping a brief-case on their knees.

When I caught up with her I asked her why she had walked away when she did. She blushed very sweetly and said, 'Well, I could see Ian sort of wrapped around you kissing the back of your neck, and I thought I would give you some privacy.'

Amazing – I could have stayed longer. . . .

A few months later, when my son, Niven, had already arranged for us to have a family visit to the crash site on 2 June, we discovered that a ten-year anniversary service was being organised by the Police Service of Northern Ireland and the military. We were delighted that all those brave people who died had not been forgotten and were only too pleased to fit into the official arrangements. It turned out to be a beautiful if sad day, an opportunity to hug and greet some of the other bereaved families, and many local people who had also had their lives disrupted in different ways by the worst peacetime air crash here came along to support us. I was pleased to be able to meet up again with old friends, most of whom I had first encountered in the immediate aftermath of the tragedy, such as the ever-welcoming lighthouse keeper and his wife. Paul, who had had the gruelling task of identifying the bodies on that awful night, was there: he was now Deputy Chief Constable of Northern Ireland. He introduced us to some of the local policewomen who had shared that terrible job and were reliving the nightmare ten years on; I hugged them and thanked them, hoping at the same time that never again will they have such a sight to remember. Of course the Reverend Roddy McNidder was there, with his warm and witty comfort, just as he had been when this awful event happened in his parish ten years before. Roddy was pleased to introduce his successor, the Reverend Martin Forrest, who made us all very welcome with just the right touch of compassion and humour. The press came along to make sure that the day was recorded, and also to remind those in government circles that the pilots' reputations have still not been officially cleared and as a result their families suffer unnecessary extra pain. During that anniversary week it was made public that John Major, the Prime Minister at the time of the crash, had stated that the official decision to blame the pilots should be reversed. I sincerely hope that the Ministry of Defence will have had the decency to apologise and exonerate these men before this book is published.

I really wanted to return to the cairn at the exact time of day that the crash had occurred. I was accompanied by Nicola and Bob, and by Gerry and Pat, the parents of my daughter-in-law Sheena, as we made our way back to the cairn for the last time. Oddly, when I had been chatting to the young soldier on duty at the gate on the way to the heather-clad hillside he told me that he feels spiritual energy in his girlfriend's house. I suggested that maybe he would feel something similar at the time of the crash that we were going down to commemorate. Nicola, with her gorgeous, witty tongue-in-cheek humour, told me not to frighten him for ever as we strode down the hill in our walking boots. Some surprise visitors also accompanied us to the site: several men and a woman in black leathers dismounted from their motorbikes as we arrived. When I asked who they were, they told me they were from the RUC (the Royal Ulster Constabulary, now renamed the Police Service of Northern Ireland), there to remember their colleagues. Seemingly, one of these fine fellows had been coming along every year to pay his respects: how great people can be in quiet ways. We joined another widow who also goes each year to the Mull, this year accompanied by a very kind friend.

Sheena's parents had not been to the site before, and I found myself almost in the role of a tour guide as I described the details of the day of the crash to them. It felt as though Ian were with me, and I was oddly at peace as I spoke. I knew that my last visit, in March, when his voice had spoken to me had given me an inner, almost serene, peace that had been earned at the end of a long ten-year journey; the pain, in spite of the unforgettable loss, had subsided at last. Love would live on for ever, but my life had moved into different dimensions in order to survive and grow. Sheena's mum, Pat, told me that she was genuinely moved, just as so many others are in this very special place. At the service earlier in the day Roddy McNidder had described this part of the Mull of Kintyre as a 'place of configuration – a place not just of pain and hurt but also a holy place'. For the people of his former parish it had become 'a place of prayer. We are not forgetting. We will not forget.' I am sure they will not, and nor will we. I remain for ever grateful to the people of that small peninsula that thrusts out into the cold North Channel of the Irish Sea for their compassion and kindness.

As our little group gathered around the cairn, just after six o'clock in the evening, the two clergymen reappeared to join us. It seemed to make a perfect group with a mixture of family old and new, colleagues old and new, the original clergyman and the present minister of the local parish – not forgetting Nicola and Bob's cute wee Skiperke dog, Ben, whom Roddy insisted on calling 'a little bear cub'.

I can see my daughter's face now as I suggested that we all circle the cairn for the ultimate time of remembrance. Her expression of 'I can't believe Mum is doing this!' increased to an 'Oh, my gawd!' face as I casually asked Roddy whether he would say a few words and suggested that perhaps we could hold hands in the circle. I heard her mutter, 'OK, but we're not dancing!' in an almost perfect reproduction of her father's expression, as the group did indeed come together to hold hands. I thought it was wonderful, and really felt the spirit of the moment. But, as is usual when I get carried away, it was not until afterwards that I realised how kind they had been to concede to a mad widow's whim!

Pat later told Sheena that the sight of her very traditional husband holding hands with a large leather-clad policeman on one side and a minister of religion on the other nearly had her in stitches, in spite of the poignancy of the day; I am sure

Ian himself would have enjoyed the sight too. I now know that they chuckle a lot up there, beyond the veil. I enjoyed it all, and appreciate the way people acted out of character to add to a special occasion. It was truly a day to be remembered with a mixture of love, sadness and laughter.

Thank you, guys.

Epilogue: Between Seix and Heaven

The future belongs to those who believe in the beauty of
their dreams.

Eleanor Roosevelt

I cannot finish writing this story without relating some of the
'signs' that have been as significant to me as the synchronicities of life. I like to think that there is a pattern to all of our
lives, and if we are searching for meanings we can always
find a sign or comfort pattern and significance that help us as
individuals to feel we are all equally important in the world.
Each one of us is here to make a contribution in our own
humble way. No one promised it would be roses all the way.
I now know that our own fear is what hurts us most – fear of
fear. There are always choices for each of us in every
situation.

The night my husband died, several things happened to a
number of people who felt that their experiences were meaningful enough to tell me about them later. Just a few days
earlier Ian had given a visitor from Cumbria a bunch of fresh
herbs and some rhubarb from our garden to take home. At
exactly the time of the helicopter crash, that person heard a
terrific crash in their farmhouse kitchen. The mirror hanging
above the fireplace had fallen to the floor and the oven had
stopped working. Nothing unusual, really – apart from the
fact that this person had hung the bunch of herbs from the

mirror to dry and Ian's rhubarb was sitting in a pie in the oven that refused to cook any more.

Similarly a friend called Gloria told me, only recently, that when she was tidying my sun-lounge a few days after the funeral a picture jumped off the wall on the other side of the room. She just said, 'Thank you, Ian' and went on with her job, after examining the hooks to see that there was no way it could have fallen by itself. He was probably saying thank you to Gloria, knowing very well that I am not very efficient at the cleaning business.

While I am on the subject of signs, something or someone is creating one right here on the page. Over the last few paragraphs that I have typed, each time I press a return key the following sentence keeps appearing on the screen in lines of three as an insertion:

Sat back to reflect what was going on
Sat back to reflect what was going back to reflect
    what was going on
Sat back to reflect what was going on

When this happened for the first time, as I worked yesterday, I decided that my computer had not really recovered from its drink of water last week (I had clumsily spilled a glass of water on to the keyboard). But today it decided to switch itself off completely and then blew a fuse in the power adapter. So just what is going on? Is it a sign? Is someone from another dimension telling me I have written enough? I can't prove it, but it is fun reflecting anyway. Fun and wisdom can be found in just about anything if we look and learn hard enough. On our life's journey we become strong when we use our inner faith to acknowledge that we can deal with everything that life throws at us. It may take time to recognise the signs, but I promise you that you will find them and they will bring comfort if you allow it to happen. When you have lost a loved one, start looking for those white feathers that let you know there is support in the Universe for you. There are almost always signs to be observed, if you use your intuition. Some people have told me that butterflies are their signal that their loved one is around them. You can ask the Universe for signs featuring items that are significant to you, and be offered a lovely surprise.

One man who used a small piece of gold plastic as a sign certainly claims to have benefited. The last time I parked my car at Malaga airport I drove into the same long-stay parking service that I had used a few weeks previously. A Spanish man came rushing out to greet me with an expression I couldn't at first fathom.

'*Señora, Señora*, you were here before, yes?'

'Yes, I was.'

'Yes, yes, and you gave me a leetle theeng, a beautiful theeng?' He was rubbing his thumb and forefinger together to demonstrate the size of the object that I had given him.

'Er . . . oh, yes. Did it come out with the change in my purse for the tip?'

'Yes, yes, it was an angel in gold!' He pronounced the word 'angel' in the Spanish way, making it sound very exotic indeed. I now knew what he was talking about, and saw that the expression on his face was tinged with tears of joy and gratitude. For several years now I have kept those small confetti sprinkles in the shape of angels in my purse. In that way, when I pay people or give someone a tip, they occasionally jump out amongst the coins. Sometimes, if people are looking really miserable, I sneak one down on the counter before I leave just in case it helps later. The pleasure that this simple act can give is a joy to witness. Some people have said that it cheers them up on a dull day, others have smiled and said, 'Just what I needed right now', and of course others (though very few) have sniffed contemptuously and shoved them directly into the bin. This lovely man, however, was telling me that a piece of confetti had had an enormous and positive effect.

'That little angel changed my whole life. I was very depressed before, and my wife too. But now our luck has changed – I will not be here when you return, because I have a better job with more wages. She is getting much better. I cannot thank you enough.'

I was so humbled by this amazing tribute. 'No, no,' I protested, 'it's not me you need to thank – it's the angels.'

'OK, but I thank you for giving me the hope and I want you to have my lucky peseta – it is very rare and old and I always carry it and now it is yours.'

It was my turn for tears in the eyes as he fished in his pocket to produce a well-rubbed peseta coin dated 1944. I was rendered quite speechless – a rare occasion for me – by this gentle man and his happy smile. Before I knew it he had deposited me outside Departures and was hugging me as I stood there in a daze of admiration for his faith. If that is what one little piece of angel-shaped gold confetti can do, just imagine what the bigger chaps in the Universe all around us can get up to if we just ask.

We start out in this life alone and we end it alone. So learning about ourselves as our own best friend is not a bad idea, sooner rather than later. We can ask for help: often the angels and spirit guides are just waiting for that. I have been told that they will not interfere until asked – rather like good friends. We cannot blame the world for our problems for ever. What did Gandhi say? 'We *are* the difference' in the world. A faith in a divine source from the larger Universe does help us feel a loving energy that we can call one of so many things, such as God, Buddha, Muhammad, good luck or our own higher self. We can feed our own soul with energy that will make us grow rather than pills that will suppress our natural flow.

Scientists are almost giving us permission to believe in other dimensions now that they are investigating their String Theory. It is just about all right these days to have love and faith in *yourself* as well as in others. If we do so, the power of the ever-present natural world will support us in our every-day life. Try it – even after a blazing row with your boss, your lover, your kids or just your carpet-wetting dog. Walk out-side into the fresh air and look up into your own piece of sky, take a deep breath and say, 'Thank you for making me, me.' Don't dwell on the negatives that let in the darkness, but look for that pinprick of light one day at a time. I promise it will soon become a big bright light that may surprise you by shining on something much bigger and brighter in your life than you ever imagined.

Need a little help? Just ask for it, and by universal law it will arrive – though perhaps not in the way that you had anticipated. It may arrive from a good friend finding just the right course for you, a truly gifted therapist, a few words in a book, a phrase caught on the radio, or a combination of all these in varying degrees. Look for the signs, the feathers and the friends, not the bottle of pills or the scapegoats to blame for your situation. Ask and you will receive: now where have I heard that before?

If enough of us take the positive steps in our own lives, with mind, body and soul, the collective consciousness of the Universe will do the rest. Life can improve for us all. We are here on earth for a reason. I know because my dead husband told me so, as have other highly respected people – living and dead, and some who have never lived at all in a human body.

On my way home from that final visit to the Mull of Kintyre to settle into my new piece of the world's space, near the beach bar called Heaven, I drove through France to see my good friends near Bergerac. I then went to look at the beautiful mountain village of Seix in the Ariège just in time to be invited to a seventieth birthday party by one of the local mountain-walking club members. This charming lady, who walks high into the Pyrenees with her friends on a regular basis, was opening her presents watched by her sixty guests as we enjoyed a delicious barbecue in the open air. It was a privilege to be included as one of only three English people in this jolly group. Her presents made me think that one day I, too, will have a home there. For her birthday she received some mountain-walking kit including a rather smart head-lamp for night use in rocky terrain. Not bad for seventy. We each have our time in the sun.

Life can indeed be a GALA if we try hard enough. Even if we just remember to be grateful for what we have and share our love with whoever needs our comfort, good things will continue to happen. We are now ready to remember and value our own ancient wisdom in our personal and environmental healing. Although it is not always immediately obvious in the grand plan of life, love and light really do make the world go round. Go on, let your spirit soar for a while, because I guarantee that no matter how low you feel there will always be someone in a worse position. Happiness is relative, and we really do all continue into a state of peace – so why not start now?

As far as my own life is concerned, I now know that there is still a lot to learn and to contribute, new people and places to visit, wonders of life and nature to marvel at and a natural curiosity to satisfy. My life is too incomplete for me to be 'settled' in any one place just yet. Settled is what we are when we feel that we are totally content with our lives, our partners, our jobs, our families. . . .

For the moment, between Seix and heaven does not seem a bad place to be.

Acknowledgements

It is no easy task to try to acknowledge everyone who has entered my life in the last ten years. So many people have contributed to my learning and renewed happiness, some without even realising it and whose names I don't even know. I would love to go back and thank those good people who just smiled at me on the way along the road, or the shop assistant who took time to pat my arm in those early days when I felt as though I were living in an emotional vacuum. I recall with warmth and gratitude the kind individuals in many gatherings who looked into my eyes, recognised some spark of sadness from their own memory and asked, 'Are you all right?'; then politely looked the other way as I murmured, 'Yes, thank you' and put on that brave face that the world needs to be reassured by. Thank you all, especially if it was you.

My wonderful children and their partners have loved and supported me through the turmoil and the calm. No one could have a more wise and loving family than Nicola, Niven, Bob, Sheena, Cian and Erin. I am truly grateful, and I love you all more than life itself. Heartfelt thanks also to my sister Pauline and Barry for always being on the end of the phone when I need you, even if Barry has developed an odd habit of calling me 'Mystic Meg'; to my nieces Rachel and Deborah for their faith in their 'mad aunty'; to Keith and Alice, Nkesha, Malika, Marcus, and Maxim, who support Rachel and Deborah as they follow their new life paths; to my parents, Bertha and Len Cheshire, for the sense of wonder in life that they shared during their lives and now in their peaceful rest beyond the veil; and to Jessie Cheshire and Doris Locke, my aunties who impress us all with their stamina and spirit.

I have made many new friends who did not know me in my 'old life' and many friends of friends, old and new, became close to me long-term or short-term and for many different reasons. They were all pieces of my spiritual and psychological jigsaw. I think the best way to thank them for their contributions to my sanity is to list them by country.

Ireland, North and South

John and Diana Sloan for long-distance love and support over the years; Michael and Christopher, who happily shared their family with me; Gloria and Roy Lowry, ever warm and faithful; the Bowes family, for fun and laughter when it was needed; the Hamilton family, for always being there with love and comfort and allowing me to use their home like a hotel when I needed a bed; Richard Barbour, my solicitor, who coped with the wrath of the government agencies and my eccentricities without losing his cool; Sam and Shirley Sinclair, who helped me plan my future when I was a weepy mess; Mary Kyle and Colette McBurney, who kept in touch and continue to remind me that there is still work to do in the deaf community; Niall Keane, Doris Nelson and Sandra O'Brien from the National Association for Deaf People in Dublin, who gave me the opportunity to make a contribution when I was still in my black hole; the Reverend George Grindle, for the wonderful funeral service and just knowing he is there; Ann Magee, who accompanied me on those early travels when we needed laughter and mutual support after our respective losses; Mandy Hannah, Joanne Maguire and William, for their friendship and all that is written here; Pat and Gerry Bradley, for their friendship and producing a beautiful daughter for my son to marry.

France

The following list could continue to infinity because of the love and friendship extended to me by so many people during my seven years there. Anne and Derek Chanter, with their friends and family; Michael and Raymond Gilbert Griffiths and Lily; Gary and Annette Ball; Jon and Chrissy Coshall; Bunty and Dave Cox; Mags and Bags Morton; Sarah and Steve Atkins; Sarah Vant; Clive and Diana Lance; Liz and Dave Rolfe; Roy and Jane Seedwell (sorry you didn't get into the film, Roy – your Irish accent wasn't good enough); Ahed and Tinike Shadid and family (thank you for the wonderful paintings with spirit presence, Tinike); Drew and Silvie Drewett; Ann-Marie and Trevor Collins; all those members of Eymet cricket club who welcomed me from 1997 onwards (not forgetting Di from Domme, who cheered me up on a very bad day); 'Stigsie' Wentworth; Julia Vidale, a neighbour in a million; Guy, Nadine and Cyril De Bortoli; Monsieur and Madame Denoux; Angelo and Claire Piazza (Angelo's artichokes continue to thrive in the garden as a memorial to this special man); Marie-Jean Kovac and Jean Paul; Maître Catherine Pratt Morton (a *notaire* with real style); Joseph and Françoise De la Mare (long may the trees support his energy downloads); Ann and John Harding, who renovated my first home in France and encouraged me to make my first professional speech for years; Louise and Didier at Ma Maison restaurant, who took the trouble to remember my granddaughter's name as a welcome guest before she had teeth or speech; Aline Trias, a therapist who works with love and universal energy; Elliette and Daniel Lacotte, the local doctor who should be an artist (even if he did call me 'the witch who lives on the hill'). Denis Boulogne, for giving so freely and generously of his time to the Bergerac angel groups; Jenny Weller, the stained-glass artist who managed so perfectly to re-create a tableau of my life in beautiful hand-blown coloured glass; Jaqui and Michel Musso, who can create miracles out of my turmoil; Scott and Judy Goodall; Les Ariègoises from the Seix walking club; Marie-Claude Carbonnel Lofts, for patiently and lovingly correcting my rotten French and supporting my endeavours to become '*une vraie vingt-quatre*' while sharing much fun and laughter.

Vancouver, British Columbia

Marion Ryan and her sons Michael and David, who opened their home and hearts to me without reservation. (Their faith in my ability to motivate others has been a special treasure to sustain me); Elizabeth and Bob Comer and family, who allowed me to hijack their house, car and cellphone while I reinvented myself as a Canadian working woman for several weeks in 2002 (their love and trust are much appreciated); and Susan and Bill James, who introduced me to the Vancouver Philharmonic Orchestra (a night to remember for ever).

Spain

June Smyth, for sharing her love and friendship so readily; the late Barry Smyth, for introducing us (somehow knowing that June and I would need each other's support in the years after his death); Neil Macfarlane, for his friendship and love for June at just the right moment in their journeys; Angela, for her helpful comments during the reading of the early drafts of this manuscript; Jason Ritchie and Iain of the Alternative World Healing circle, for their fellowship, warm welcome and fun as they walk powerfully towards spreading love, light and happiness on the Costa del Sol. William and James Tomlinson from Telefonica in English, who helped me to get back on line to deliver the manuscript just in time for the deadline; Dr Wu Hang for expert acupuncture; Elaine, for helping me to celebrate that final typed word.

Angel friends from all over the place

Diana Cooper, for helping me to see outside of the box of grief that confines us all; Heike Rann, for loyal friendship; Jane Cull; Margaret; Silvie Turner, for expanding my consciousness even more; Rita Hansford, with thanks for the fun and laughter and hundreds of cups of coffee (not to mention the champagne) during the early chapters of the manuscript on that sun-filled Hawaiian terrace; Sandra and Marie-Louise, for the medicine wheel; Steven Graham, for introducing me to Yogananda; Jo and Bobby, who fell in love with angels and each other at the same time (it was a pleasure to behold, and I don't apologise for the match-making!); Lynne Starke from Hawaii, for her commitment to therapeutic Watsu massage, bringing help to many along her path; Kevin Barker, for friendship and wise words at just the right time.

England and Scotland

Huge thanks to all those old friends too numerous to mention who know they have quietly supported me even when I forget to ring or write for many months. Bruce and Mary

Acknowledgements

Beresford, who opened their home and hearts to my family whenever needed; Alastair, for words of support and the memorable lunch at which Ian came to say hello by stopping my watch for the whole time that we were speaking of him; the members of ELMS (Escape Lines Memorial Society), for introducing me to the brave and the bold across generations.

My original publisher, Roland Philipps, from Hodder & Stoughton who believed in me after reading only a few weird ideas of the early script; Rowena Webb, who accepted and supported the idea, much to my initial surprise. Her humour and compassion helped me greatly as I struggled to write for the first time about me rather than other people. Helen Coyle, my lovely editor, who patiently accepted my very direct and probing questions as we discovered a rapport over our first lunch meeting. Thank you for the guidance and for beating my waffle into shape.

*Last but not least I sincerely thank the spirit of
Ian Phoenix who came back to motivate
me into the action that is this book.
May he rest in peace wherever and however he chooses.*

Further Reading

These are just a few of the books that have inspired and encouraged me at various times during the last ten years:

Bloom, William, *Working with Angels*, Piatkus, 1998

Bloom, William, *The Endorphin Effect: a breakthrough strategy for holistic health and spiritual wellbeing*, Piatkus, 2001

Boryensko, Joan, *Minding the Body, Mending the Mind*, Addison-Wesley, 1987

Brennan, Barbara Ann, *Hands of Light*, Bantam, 1988

Brennan, Barbara Ann, *Light Emerging: the journey of personal healing*, Bantam, 1993

Bruyere, Rosalyn, *Wheels of Light: a study of the chakras*, Bon Productions, Arcadia, CA, 1989

Chopra, Deepak, *Quantum Healing*, Bantam, 1989

Chopra, Deepak, *Ageless Body, Timeless Mind*, Harmony Books, 1993

Chopra, Deepak, *Perfect Health*, Harmony Books, 2001

Chopra, Deepak, *The Seven Spiritual Laws of Success*, Bantam, 1996

Choquette, Sonia, *Diary of a Psychic: shattering the myths*, Hay House, 2003

Choquette, Sonia, *Trust Your Vibes: secret tools for six sensory living*, Hay House, 2004

Cockell, Jenny, *Yesterday's Children*, Piatkus, 1993

Coelho, Paul, *Manual of the Warrior of Light*, HarperCollins, 2002

Cooper, Diana, *The Power of Inner Peace*, Piatkus, 1994

Cooper, Diana, *A Little Light on Ascension*, Findhorn, 1997

Cooper Diana, *A Little Light on the Spiritual Laws*, Hodder & Stoughton, 2000

Cooper, Diana, *Angel Inspiration*, Hodder & Stoughton, 2001

Darling, Wayne 'Lone Eagle', *Fifth Dimensional Healing: crystal wis-*

dom and the five elements of multidimensional healing, Words of Wizdom Books, 1998

Dinawa, *Sacred History and Earth Prophecies*, In Print Publishing, Sedona, AZ, 1996

Dolan, Mia, *The Gift: the story of an ordinary woman's extraordinary power*, Element, 2003

Dowding, Air Vice Marshal H., *Many Mansions*, London, 1943

Emery, Marcia, *The Intuitive Healer: how to get in touch with your own healing power*, Thorsons, 1999

George, Chief Dan, *My Heart Soars*, Hancock House, 1974

Guirdham, Arthur, *The Cathars and Reincarnation*, Spearman, 1970

Hall, Judy, *The Crystal Bible: a definitive guide to crystals*, Godsfield, 2003

Hall, Nicola, *Reflexology, a Step by Step Guide*, Element, 1997

Hoff, Benjamin, *The Tao of Pooh*, Penguin, 1982

Jung, Carl G. et al., *Man and His Symbols*, Doubleday, New York, 1964

Lawrence, Richard, *The Meditation Plan: 21 keys to your inner potential*, Piatkus, 1999

Lovelock, James, *The Ages of Gaia: a biography of the earth*, Oxford University Press, 1988

McDermott, Ian and Joseph O'Connor, *NLP and Health: practical ways to bring mind and body into harmony*, Thorsons, 1996

McGerr, Angela, *A Harmony of Angels*, Quadrille, 2001

Myss, Caroline, *Anatomy of the Spirit: the seven stages of power and healing*, Bantam, 1997

Myss, Caroline, *Sacred Contracts: awakening your divine potential*, Harmony Books, 2001

Newton, Michael, *Destiny of Souls: new case studies of life between lives*, Llewellyn Publications, 2004

Pasricha, Satwant, *Claims of Reincarnation: an empirical study of cases in India*, Harman Publishing, New Delhi, 1990

Radin, D. I., *The Conscious Universe: the scientific truth of psychic phenomena*, Harper Edge, New York, 1997

Redfield, James, *The Celestine Prophecy*, Warner Books, New York, 1994

Schaufelberger-Landherr, Edith, *The Power of Stones*, Edith Schaufelberger, 1992

Servan-Schreiber, Dr David, *Healing without Freud or Prozac: natural* approach to curing stress, anxiety and depression without drugs and without psychoanalysis, Rodale, 2003

Sha, Dr Zhi Gang, *Power Healing: the four keys to energising your body, mind and spirit*, HarperCollins, 2003

Stemman, Roy, *Reincarnation: true stories of past lives*, Piatkus, 1997

Stone, Joshua, *Soul Psychology: keys to ascension*, Light Technology Publishing, Sedona, AZ, 1994

Stone, Joshua, *Beyond Ascension: how to complete the seven levels of initiation*, Light Technology Publishing, Sedona, AZ, 1995

Stormer, Chris, *Language of the Feet: what feet can tell you*, Hodder & Stoughton, 1995

Sun Bear, Wabun Wind and Crysalis Mulligan, *Dancing with the Wheel: the medicine wheel workbook*, Simon & Schuster, 1991

Virtue, Doreen, *Chakra Clearing: awakening your spiritual power to know and heal* (including an excellent CD), Hay House, 1998

Wallace, Robert, *The Neurophysiology of Enlightenment*, Maharishi International University Press, 1991

Webster, Richard, *Aura Reading for Beginners*, Llewellyn Publications, 1998

Weiss, Brian, *Many Lives, Many Masters*, Piatkus, 1994

Weiss, M. D., *Through Time into Healing: discovering the power of regression therapy to erase trauma and transform mind – body relationships*, Touchstone, 1993

Worwood, Valerie Ann, *The Fragrant Heavens: the spiritual dimensions of fragrance and aromatherapy*, Bantam, 1999

Yogananda, Paramahansa, *Autobiography of a Yogi*, Self Realisation Fellowship, 1946

Young, Jacqueline, *Acupressure: the oriental way to health*, Thorsons, 1994

HODDER
MOBIUS

Transform your life
with Hodder Mobius

For the latest information on the best in
Spirituality, Self-Help,
Health & Wellbeing and Parenting,

visit our website
www.hoddermobius.com